Mystery of the Island Jewels

by Joyce A. Stengel

Aladdin Paperbacks
New York London Toronto Sydney Singapore

First Aladdin Paperbacks edition May 2002

ALADDIN PAPERBACKS
An imprint of Simon & Schuster
Children's Publishing Division
1230 Avenue of the Americas
New York, NY 10020

Designed by Debra Sfetsios
The text of this book was set in Garamond Three.
Printed in the United States of America
2 4 6 8 10 9 7 5 3

Library of Congress Control Number: 2001053441

ISBN 0-689-85049-2

For Bob

my husband and friend

with love

Chapter 1

Cassie Hartt stumbled over Lisa's shoes as she hurried from their stateroom. Wish I had my own cabin, she thought, pulling the door shut.

Her straw bag's strap caught in the door. She yanked at it, but it didn't budge. "I'll never get up on deck to talk with Dad alone—before Lisa or Sonya get to him," she muttered, fumbling in her pocket for her key.

Cassie freed the strap, locked the door, and started down the narrow hall. Ahead of her a door flew open and a tall, dark-haired boy rushed out. "Larson," he called to the steward who was leaving the room next to his, "my room's been searched. Things are out of place."

Larson strode to his side. "I cleaned your room

earlier. Maybe I moved your stuff."

Gorgeous, Cassie thought, checking out the boy in the doorway. Bet he plays basketball. He looks about fifteen, maybe sixteen, just a little older than me.

The steward, in his uniform of white slacks and shirt, didn't look much older than the boy and was the same height, but more muscular. He stood with his arms folded across his chest, leaning back on his heels.

The boy ran his hand through his dark hair. "But someone went through my bureau," he said.

"Not me."

"Well, someone did."

"Was anything taken?"

"No."

Larson shrugged, dismissing the matter.

As Cassie walked toward them, she felt Larson's bold eyes sweeping from her auburn ponytail to her bare feet. Her face burned. His look made her uncomfortably aware of her changing figure.

She hurried past the boys, putting the scene and her curiosity about it from her mind. She wanted to see her father, talk to him—just the two of them.

Clambering up the stairs to the sundeck, she passed the lifeboat platform, the commodore deck, and the bridge deck. Yesterday, she'd explored the ship. Alone. It had been a nonstop day. Flying from Maine to Miami. Meeting her father and his new family. Boarding the ship. She and her stepsister, twelve-year-old Lisa Mason, left in their cabin. Her father and Sonya—Cassie couldn't think of her as her father's wife—settling into theirs.

An awkward silence had fallen between Cassie and Lisa. To relieve it, Cassie had proposed that they explore the ship. But Lisa had said no. So Cassie had gone by herself. She'd maneuvered through the hallways crowded with people finding their staterooms. She'd gotten lost on every deck, found the swimming pools, peeked in the casino and lounges. She'd felt lonely, left out amidst all the busy, happy chatter.

Cassie usually made friends easily. It hadn't taken her long to meet people when she and her mother and her little brother, Danny, had moved to Maine last year. She smiled now, remembering the adventures she'd had last summer as she had helped solve a mystery in her new town, Kittiwake Bay. It had been exciting—but scary, too.

Well, all that was behind her now. She blinked hard and reminded herself to make more of an effort with Lisa and Sonya. But now she was looking for a chance to talk to her father. Just the two of them. Her stomach knotted. What could they say to each other now that they were face-to-face, after all this time?

She tugged open the heavy door to the sundeck and stepped into blazing heat. She searched the lounge chairs, spotted her father, his rangy, six-foot frame hunched over something he held in his hands. As she got closer, she noticed his sandy-gray hair was thinning on top.

Cassie stopped dead when she saw Lisa sitting on the other side of a small table. Lisa threw down a card, laughed, and scooped up the cards, then reached for a bag of M&M's.

Tears of disappointment stung Cassie's eyes. Angrily, she brushed them away and searched in her bag for sunglasses. Why was Lisa there?

At first, Cassie hadn't wanted to come on this cruise with her father and his new family. She felt that she hardly knew him. He'd always been busy with his law practice before he and her mother divorced. But she had let her mother convince her, hoping, somewhere deep inside, that her father did love her, and that on the cruise they'd get to know each other. But they hadn't even talked, not really. Sonya and Lisa were always there.

James Hartt looked up from the cards Lisa dealt him and peered at Cassie over his half-glasses. "Hey, Cassie, how about a game of set-back?" he said.

Cassie's bare feet burned on the sun-scorched deck. "I don't know how to play," she murmured.

"Lisa will teach you. She's killing me. How about it, Lisa?"

Lisa wiped her hands on a towel, then reached for the Pepsi by her chair. Her long blond hair swung back, exposing her full face as she guzzled the soda. "Yuk. This is warm," she complained.

James Hartt scooped up the cards and shuffled them. He began to deal three hands. "We each get six cards, right, Lisa?"

Lisa reached for more M&M's. "I don't want to play anymore," she said.

Cassie pulled boat shoes from her bag, slipped them on, and dropped the bag to the deck. "I thought you were going shopping with your mother, Lisa."

Lisa glared at her. "I decided not to." She swung her plump legs into the lounge chair, settled back, and closed her eyes.

Cassie noted the bulging briefcase by her father's chair. Had he brought work with him on the cruise? "What's in the briefcase, Dad?"

James Hartt patted the smooth leather, leaving a damp imprint of his big, bony hand. "Papers I have to look over. I have an appointment in San Juan to take a deposition. I've been trying to get hold of this man for months. It just so happens he'll be in San Juan the same day the ship docks there. Then he's flying off to some other country. His testimony could be vital to a very big case."

Lisa, without opening her eyes, said, "But, Daddy Jim promised to play cards with me first."

Cassie rolled her eyes. "Daddy Jim," she thought, give me a break. Not sure what to do, Cassie stood, chewing her lower lip, looking from her father to Lisa.

Her father pulled his briefcase to his lap and pulled out some papers. He glanced up at Cassie, his left hand shielding his eyes from the sun. "Pull over a chair, Cassie. Relax."

His manner was short, preoccupied. She didn't want to stay. How could she escape? Then she saw the dark-haired boy.

Cassie's eyes swept to her father. Anger flared through her. He had time to play cards with Lisa, but no time for her. She made a split-second decision. Grabbing her bag, she said, "I'm going in."

Engrossed in his papers, he didn't answer. Cassie turned on her heel and left.

Chapter 2

She caught up with the boy on the inner deck. "Hi," she said. "I heard you talking to Larson. Did someone really steal something from your room?" She felt her face flush, aware that she had pounced on a complete stranger.

The boy's dark eyebrows drew together in a frown. "No. Nothing was missing, but someone was messing around the room."

"Why would anyone do that?" she asked, falling into step beside him.

The boy shrugged. "Beats me. You going to the lecture on gems and superstitions too?"

Gems and superstitions? Why not? thought Cassie. She nodded. He pulled the heavy glass door to the Rainbow Lounge open, and a blast of cold air hit them.

Cassie's eyes adjusted to the dimness of the room, where a man lectured from the small dance floor. He was of medium height, with deep-set eyes, a broad nose, a long upper lip, and a second chin beginning to show. His thin neck and sloping shoulders made his head look too large. He frowned at the latecomers as they slid into seats; tenting his fingers, he continued speaking.

"Superstition isn't limited to gemstones. Why, on the island of Martinique, where we dock in a few days, there's a place called Maiden's Hill." He paused. "It's said to be haunted. The story behind it is a bloody and romantic one."

Cassie, intrigued, sat forward on the edge of her chair.

"Centuries ago, before Columbus sailed the oceans, the Arawaks lived on the Caribbean Islands. They were a peaceful people. They loved their children and old people, and the men treated their women with respect.

"In the thirteen hundreds, fierce, battle-hungry Carib Indians invaded the islands. The Caribs were as violent as the Arawaks were peaceful. They were cannibals. They didn't kill the young boys at first. They castrated them and fattened them up for feasts. And they didn't kill the women at all. They used them as slaves and to breed future warriors."

The man looked around the quiet room. He had everyone's full attention. "The story goes that the Caribs stole over the rugged eastern mountains and attacked the Arawaks who were playing a game on a level plateau high above the calm sea. They played with a rubber ball on a cleared area about the size of a football field. Each team had a goal that the other team tried to drive the ball across. Sounds like our games, doesn't it? Football, soccer."

The lecturer cleared his throat and took a sip of water from a glass on a nearby table. "The game was part of the celebration of the champion player having selected a mate. She, a young maiden, and the other villagers watched the players and cheered them on."

Cassie's mind wandered. A young maiden. How old? Fourteen—my age? A girl in a bright garment, black hair with white flowers woven through it streaming down her back. Dark eyes glowing as she watched her future husband—her mate. He would play a magnificent game for her, his muscles rippling beneath smooth brown skin.

The professor's voice drew Cassie back to the present.

"On this particular day, the savage Caribs swept down from the mountains and slaughtered the Arawaks. The story goes that the Carib chief caught sight of the Arawak champion hurrying the young maiden to a cave. With a bloodcurdling cry, he sprang after them, slaying the man with a murderous blow of his club. The Carib then disappeared into the cave to retrieve his prize."

Cassie, eyes wide, hands clenched into tight fists, willed the Arawak girl to escape.

A note of dread entered the professor's voice. "But neither of them came out. Eventually, the conquering warriors searched the cave for their leader and the girl. They found their chief with a fire-hardened wooden dagger in his heart." He stopped and gazed into space. Cassie saw him rub, with the three middle fingers of his right hand, a gold ring on his middle left finger.

Clearing his throat, he turned his deep-set gaze back to the audience. "They never found the maiden. Through the centuries people have reported hearing a piercing scream, supposedly that of the dying Arawak, then seeing the ghostly figure of a young girl coming from the cave and roaming the hill."

Cassie's heart pounded. The hair on the back of

her neck prickled. The girl had killed the Carib and come back, night after night, through all the long years, mourning her lost love.

There was silence, then a murmur rippled through the audience. Cassie sighed. She knew, she just knew, how that Arawak maiden felt. She nudged the boy sitting beside her. "Wouldn't it be great to visit that hill?" she whispered.

The boy nodded, then put a finger to his lips, signaling her to be quiet, for the lecturer was speaking again.

"Well, back to what I was talking about before the question on superstition. Gemstones. There's a great deal of superstition related to them, too. They seem to have had religious or spiritual significance in all human societies. . . ."

Cassie picked up a brochure left on a chair. Philippe Ornard, author of two books: *Gemstones—Their Mystical Power and Symbolism,* and *Superstitions of the Caribbean*. Writer; professor of gemology.

An older woman asked, "Do you believe in those powers, Professor Ornard?"

The woman's question brought Cassie's attention back to Philippe Ornard. He doesn't look like a professor, she thought. Maybe it's those wild floral shorts and that bright green shirt.

Professor Ornard stroked his gold ring, tilted his head down, and fixed his gaze on the woman. "Do I believe in what powers, ma'am?"

Cassie saw the woman flush. She then uncrossed her legs and straightened her shoulders. "Why, the magic, the mystical quality of jewels you've been talking about."

The man continued to gaze at her, then said, "Let me answer your question this way, ma'am: I believe in the power of belief." He pointed to the stack of books ready for autographing and purchase. "Read my book," he intoned. "Read my book and you'll discover how persuasive that power can be."

The woman settled back in her chair. Cassie looked from her to the professor, who stood gazing into space, absently tapping a fingernail against his ring.

"I'd say you believe, Professor," challenged a man sitting in the front row.

Professor Ornard's head bobbed toward the speaker. He straightened up and rubbed his palms against his shorts. "What's that?" he barked.

The gray-haired, bespectacled man pointed to the professor's left hand. "I said, I think you believe those silly superstitions. Isn't that an ankh on your left hand—that ring you keep touching?"

The professor's right hand automatically went to the ring. He shrugged and stretched his face into a smile. "You're very observant, sir." He held up his hand. "Yes, this is an ankh, my talisman, my good-luck piece. I think most of you will agree we can all use a little good luck."

A twitter of laughter swept through the audience. Cassie glanced down at the deep green emerald on her little finger. Her father had given it to her on her ninth birthday. She twisted it; the gold bit into her finger. She wondered if her father remembered giving it to her. "To bring out the green in your eyes," he had said.

Professor Ornard's deep voice rumbled on. "Speaking of luck, a great deal of superstition surrounds the lost Jeweled Jesu."

"What's the Jeweled Jesu?" a man called out.

Professor Ornard held up one of his books. "It is or was a rare and beautiful piece. It's pictured here on the cover of my book."

Cassie could see a silver statue of Christ on the Cross against a background of blue. An inverted U of colors seemed to encircle Him.

"No one knows exactly when this beautiful work was created. It is believed that it dates back to the days when Spain ruled the Caribbean.

"If you look at the picture closely, you will see

the intricate detail. The piece is valued not only for its silver but also for the jewels surrounding the statue." He paused and, holding the large book in his left hand, followed the inverted U of colors with his right forefinger. Cassie could hear the scraping of his nail against the hard cover.

"Why do you say 'is or was a rare and beautiful piece'?" the man asked.

"Because it has been missing since Mount Pelée, the volcano in Martinique, erupted in nineteen hundred and two—exactly one hundred years ago. The statue—"

"Mon Dieu," the boy next to Cassie breathed. Then, leaning forward, he asked, "When did you say that volcano erupted?"

"Nineteen hundred and two, young man. Why do you ask?" Philippe Ornard tented his fingers and stared at the boy.

What are they so tense about? Cassie wondered. She noticed the professor didn't tap his fingers together now but pressed them, knuckle-white, against each other.

The boy sat back in his chair. "No reason," he murmured. "Just curious." He glanced sideways toward Cassie, then frowned.

For the first time, Cassie wondered why he had come to this lecture. A quick survey of the audience showed her that they were the only young people. She had wanted to escape her father and Lisa. What was the boy's reason? She stole a glance at his set face and saw his Adam's apple bob in his throat.

Cassie noticed that the professor kept glancing at the boy as he finished his explanation. "As I was saying. The statue stood on the altar of a church near Saint-Pierre, which was the capital of Martinique at the time. The town was destroyed when the volcano burst, but this particular church, on a rise of land far from town, was not. It was badly damaged, but many artifacts were recovered. The Jeweled Jesu, however, was not one of them. Neither it nor any of the stones has ever been found."

He poured himself another glass of water, drank deeply, and continued. "Sacrilegious though it would be, considering the mystical power of the stones, some believe that it was dismantled and sold for the value of its silver and jewels." Ornard looked ruefully at the picture, sighed, and placed the book on the table.

Before she realized she was thinking it, Cassie blurted, "What kind of mystical powers did the stones have?"

The professor's eyes pierced her. "Each of the

twelve stones represents one of the apostles, and each stone is said to have a power of its own. The power or magic is presumed to influence the affairs of men. That is why the superstitious say that whoever has the statue will suffer ill luck. On Martinique, when a family experiences misfortune, people say, 'Their ancestors must have stolen the Jeweled Jesu, and the sins of the father are being visited on the child.' Superstition?" Philippe Ornard paused, slid his eyes to the gray-haired, bespectacled man, then said, "Perhaps, but . . ." He shrugged his shoulders and pursed his lips.

Cassie hugged her arms to her chest, cold in the air-conditioned room. I'd love to find that statue, she thought, unaware of the group breaking up around her. Just think, a treasure. I would return it to the church of Martinique for everyone to admire. What would my father say then? We'll be in Martinique in a few days. What if . . .

The boy stood up and stretched. Cassie tapped his arm. "What does that word 'ankh' actually mean? Do you know?"

The boy spoke quietly as they wandered up to the table. "It's an ancient Egyptian symbol of eternal life, a cross with a loop at the top."

A few people were looking through Professor

Ornard's books. Cassie studied the picture of the delicately wrought and jeweled silver band that nearly encircled the Jesu. She recognized a few of the twelve stones: sapphire, amethyst, topaz, and, there it was—an emerald. "I wonder what power the emerald has," she murmured, wriggling her nose.

Professor Ornard autographed a book, handed it to a woman, then turned to them. "You're the boy who wanted to know when Mount Pelée erupted. Did that date have some special meaning for you?"

The boy's left brow arched, and he shrugged his shoulders. "No, not really. I have relatives on Martinique. In fact, my mother was born there, and I remember her talking about the volcano, even though it erupted before she was born."

"So . . . you're returning to Martinique for a visit?"

"No. I've never been there before. I'm going to visit my grandfather on his plantation."

Cassie was studying the professor's ring. It looked worn. Probably because he rubs it so much, she thought.

"Your grandfather? What is your name, young man?"

"Charles," said the boy.

"Charles what?" The man insisted.

"Charles Reyes."

"And your grandfather's name? I know many of the plantation owners."

"My grandfather is Jerome Nobre."

"I don't believe I have the pleasure of knowing him."

"I wonder if you could tell me about my ring—" Charles fingered a chain around his neck.

"And mine," Cassie interrupted, holding out her hand with the emerald.

A crew member hurried over and slapped Professor Ornard on the shoulder. "Phil, I hear you had to have a special escort to the ship."

Cassie caught an annoyed look on the professor's face.

"Yes," he said. "I missed the plane to Miami."

"Glad you made it. I'd like to go over your schedule . . . unless you're busy," he added, nodding toward Charles and Cassie.

"I'm busy," answered the professor, turning away from them.

Cassie and Charles drifted out of the lounge to the nearly deserted sundeck. The late afternoon sun hung low in the western sky. Cassie took a deep breath of the salty air and rubbed her arms to warm herself up after the frigid temperature in the lounge. She reached into her bag for her sunglasses. Her eyes fell to the deck chairs where her father and Lisa had been sitting.

"He was rude, don't you think? Turning away from us like that?" said Cassie.

"Kind of." Charles patted a lump beneath his blue-and-white shirt. "I wanted to ask him about this ring. But . . . by the way, what's your name?"

"Cassie Hartt." She looked at the gold chain disappearing under Charles's collar. "How come you wear your ring on a chain?"

"It's too big."

Cassie leaned against the railing. "Do you believe that story about Maiden's Hill?" she asked.

Charles turned his dark gaze on her. "Do I believe in ghosts, you mean? I've read about parapsychology, but—"

"Para what?"

"Parapsychology. It's the study of psychic phenomena. Ghosts. Hauntings. Some people believe a violent death can cause a spirit to linger at the site, but . . . I doubt it. No, I guess I don't believe in ghosts."

With an intake of breath, Cassie caught her lower lip with her teeth. "But it could be true. There could really be a ghost of Maiden's Hill!

Wouldn't it be great to go there? To see for ourselves?" she whispered, eyes wide.

A smile twitched at the corners of Charles's mouth and lightened his somber eyes.

"Has your mother ever mentioned Maiden's Hill?" Cassie asked, freeing a strand of red-gold hair that was caught in her glasses.

A veil dropped over Charles's eyes, and he shifted from foot to foot. "My mother is dead. She was killed in an automobile accident last year. A drunken driver smashed into her car."

Cassie saw the pain in his dark eyes. "Oh, I'm sorry," she whispered, gently touching his arm. She thought of her own mother. Busy with work and classes but always there when Cassie needed her. And her father—the hurt, the loss after the divorce. But dead—that, she couldn't imagine.

After a moment, Charles continued. "My father—he hasn't been the same since. He was going to come with me. But at the last minute he had to go on a business trip. That's why I'm on this cruise instead of just flying there."

Cassie heard the grief in his voice. He turned toward the sea and grabbed the railing with both hands.

"Look," Cassie said impulsively, "why don't you eat with us if you're traveling alone?"

Charles hesitated. "I don't know . . . anyway, my cousin's boarding the ship in Puerto Rico."

Cassie smiled. "He can eat with us too."

"But . . . what about your family?"

"You'd really be doing me a big favor. I'm not here with my family. What I mean is"—Cassie hesitated—"I'm here to get to know my father's new wife and her daughter. And we're supposed to be great friends. And . . . well, I hardly know my father anymore. I haven't seen him in over a year. Once-a-week phone calls. Sunday afternoon like clockwork . . ." Cassie's voice trailed off. She raised her eyebrows, pulled her lips to one side, and held her hands out in a helpless gesture.

"Okay." Charles laughed. "You've convinced me."

Cassie smiled again, liking the way his laugh lit up his whole face.

Chapter 3

Cassie woke with a start. The sound of Lisa's even breathing filled the cabin. Cassie peered at the alarm clock, its numbers glowing in the dim light. Plenty of time before breakfast. She lay back and stretched, then threw the light blanket off and knelt on the narrow cot. Holding the heavy gray curtain back, she squinted at the sun striking blindly down, its rays bouncing off the water. Dust motes tickled her nose and made her sneeze.

Lisa moaned and pulled the sheet over her face. "Shut the curtain. My eyes hurt," she complained.

Cassie let the drape fall into place, then swung her long legs over the edge of the bed. Scenes from last night flashed through her mind as she washed in the cramped shower. Her father's noncommittal welcome when she brought Charles to the table. Lisa, unable to take her eyes off Charles, and Sonya, prattling on and on.

The water pressure dropped, and an icy stream blasted her, raising goose bumps. After toweling dry, she pulled on denim shorts and a yellow blouse.

Rummaging through the pile on the bureau for her key, she knew she'd been right to suggest they divide the space in the tiny cabin. Now she couldn't find her key. Lisa's mess—candy wrappers, hair bands, gum—was already flowing over the dividing line.

Cassie retrieved her key from under a candy wrapper and slid it into her shorts pocket. "You'd better get up soon or you'll miss breakfast, Lisa."

Lisa stretched and yawned. She stared at Cassie but said nothing.

"See you later," Cassie called. The door clicked behind her. She bounded down the hall, glad to get away from Lisa's unfriendly gaze.

Cassie flew down the four flights of stairs to the Columbus Dining Room on the main deck. Away from Lisa, she felt lighter.

She wondered if Sonya and her father would be

at the breakfast table already. Was her father angry that she had invited Charles to eat with them? She never knew what he was thinking. Last night, he had seemed friendly enough, but she thought she had detected a hint of irritation. Maybe today they could talk.

Today would be better. She would really try to make friends with Sonya. Sonya was nothing like her own mother. Her mother was a nurse, studying to become a nurse practitioner. Sonya did something with colors—a color consultant, she said. Whatever that was.

Cassie held open the door to the dining room for an elderly couple. Cold air drifted from the immense, air-conditioned room. She stood a moment to get her bearings, taking in the grandeur of the room, with its maroon carpet, maroon-and-blue striped chairs, white linen tablecloths, and crystal chandeliers.

She started for their table near the center. Charles caught her eye and waved. Her father and Sonya were also there.

Cassie slipped into her chair and scooted it up to the table. "Morning," she said, smiling at Charles.

"Hi," Charles said, smiling back as though relieved that she was there. He passed her a plate of breakfast breads. She took a cinnamon bun and watched him take two.

Her father glanced up from his newspaper and lifted his eyes over his reading glasses. Cassie noticed the furrows on his forehead and the firm contour of his jaw. Her mother's voice sounded in her ear: "Your jaw line is just like your father's. Guess that's who you get that stubborn streak from."

"Morning, Cassie," he said, then disappeared behind the paper.

Sonya looked up from the daily itinerary that was slipped under their door each morning. Her glossy pink lips smiled brightly at Cassie. "They're having that lecture on gemstones again. Maybe I'll go to that." A frown creased her forehead. "Where is Enrico with the coffee? Honestly, you'd think the service would be better," she complained, her well-manicured fingers playing restlessly with the silver.

Pampered hands, thought Cassie, comparing them unfavorably with her mother's strong, capable hands. Poor Enrico, she moaned inwardly. She looked at the busboy, who was serving coffee at the next table. His meaty but deft hands were constantly busy—setting or clearing tables, filling water glasses, pouring coffee.

"Enrico," Sonya called in her light chirping

voice as the harried man turned from the other table. "Coffee, please. We need coffee here."

Lisa walked up to the table and slumped into the empty chair. "What's for breakfast?" She opened her menu and yawned loudly.

"Cover your mouth, dear," Sonya admonished. She sipped her coffee and wrinkled her nose. "Bitter, must be the dregs." She raised her voice. "Enrico." The man hurried back to the table. "Fresh coffee, please. Be a dear and make us a fresh pot."

Sonya turned her attention back to the itinerary. "Who wants to join me in the Ship Shape fitness program? Let's see—there's also Yoga and Aquadynamics."

Lisa drank a glass of orange juice. "Daddy Jim and I have to finish our set-back tournament."

Sonya's voice pitched higher. "James, you aren't listening."

Cassie knew her father hadn't been listening. She remembered that preoccupied look from before—when he and her mother were still married.

James folded the paper and placed it on the table, removed his half-glasses, and pinched the bridge of his nose. "Sorry, Sonya. I've got a lot to do today. Puerto Rico tomorrow. You know I've got that deposition to get ready for."

Lisa took a spoonful of peanut butter and spread it thickly on her toast. "But, Daddy Jim, you promised to play cards with me today," she whined.

Cassie saw the tiny annoyed frown between her father's eyes. It looked like Lisa wouldn't always get her way.

Suddenly his gaze softened. "I did promise, didn't I? Tell you what. If I get right to work after breakfast, I should have some free time this afternoon." Turning to Cassie and Charles, he added, "What do you say, Cassie? Charles? The four of us will have a game."

Cassie steeled herself against the hurt. Anger bubbled in her. Just last night, after dinner, she'd asked her father to walk around the deck with her. Ten minutes. That's all. But there hadn't been time.

Cassie kept her voice expressionless. "Charles and I have made other plans."

"I'd like you to play cards with us, Cassie," her father insisted.

Cassie bristled at the demanding tone. Hazel eyes stared into hazel eyes.

"Who's that?" Lisa's voice cut off Cassie's angry retort. "What a wild outfit. And look at those hairy legs. And his toenails. Gross."

"Lisa," said Sonya. "That's not proper table talk."

Everyone turned to see the man who had stopped to visit at a nearby table. Cassie's eyes fell to his feet. Thick, yellow nails jutted off the edge of his sandals.

"It's Professor Ornard," said Charles.

Sonya's face lit up. "Professor Ornard. We should talk to him."

To Cassie's surprise, her father stopped the professor as he passed their table.

Sonya chirped, "You're giving another lecture today, Professor? I'd love to hear you. Such an interesting topic—gemstones. Gems are so beautiful. All those colors. Every hue of the rainbow. You know, I advise people, in my line of work, as to which gems they should wear."

Philippe Ornard's deep-set eyes slid from Sonya to Cassie, then to Charles. "Ah, here's the young lady and gentleman who were at my lecture yesterday." His heavy voice had a coaxing quality.

Sonya gestured to Cassie's emerald. "You see, Professor, Cassie's wearing an emerald, which is a perfect color for her."

Philippe Ornard cast a cursory glance at the ring. "Yes. Yes, indeed," he said.

James Hartt spoke. "Cassie and Charles were

telling us about the Jeweled Jesu last night. It sounds like a beautiful piece."

The professor's big head swiveled toward him. The tips of his right three middle fingers tapped his gold ankh. "Yes. A beautiful piece. Most likely lost forever."

Fernando, the plump, dark-skinned waiter, clattered a tray filled with bowls of fresh fruit onto a serving stand. Cassie, startled, glanced up and saw him cross himself.

Her father turned in his chair. "Up too late, Fernando?"

Fernando's full cheeks darkened. He laughed apologetically. "I'm sorry, sir. No. I wasn't up late. I heard you say 'Jeweled Jesu.'" Again, he crossed himself.

The professor eyed him sharply. "Ah. You know of the Jeweled Jesu?"

While Fernando deftly served the fruit, he explained. "I am from Martinique. There, rumors circulate. They say that many years ago the Jeweled Jesu was stolen. That one day it will turn up. But, until it once again sits on the altar of God, much unhappiness will surround it."

Somewhere in the back of her mind, Cassie noted Enrico poised at the serving station, listening.

"Excuse me."

Everyone turned to look at the crew member standing at the back of Lisa's chair.

The man cleared his throat importantly. "I have a faxed message for Mr. Charles Nobre Reyes." He raised his eyebrows quizzically.

Charles's head shot up. "I'm Charles Reyes," he said, reaching for the paper with a trembling hand.

Charles read the message. His face went white. "My grandfather," he whispered. "My grandfather is dead."

Chapter 4

Professor Ornard's heavy head swiveled toward Charles. Beads of perspiration dotted his forehead. Cassie heard him murmer, "Nobre Reyes. So—you are the one."

As a buzz of sympathy rounded the table, Cassie looked from the professor to Charles. She put a hand on his arm, dry and cool in the air-conditioned room. "Oh, Charles. How awful," she murmured.

Charles's left hand grasped the fabric of his shirt and the ring beneath it. He pulled the ring out. Heavy gold with a red stone. Head bent, he studied it. "He wanted me to bring it . . . to explain . . ."

James Hartt reached over and put a comforting hand on Charles's shoulder. "You've had a shock, Charles. Would you like to go back to your stateroom?"

Charles, his eyes bright with unshed tears, nodded. "Excuse me, please," he said, his voice barely audible.

The professor, clenching his left hand with his right, watched him go. "Terrible news," he said. He turned and bent his gaze on Cassie. "Young Charles mentioned his ring to me yesterday. You tell him, young lady, I'll be glad to look at it. Oh, and your ring, too. Yes, come see me this afternoon, and I'll tell you both about your rings." He nodded to everyone at the table and left.

Cassie watched the professor walk away. Why had he said he'd look at their rings? He hadn't wanted to bother with them yesterday. He probably felt sorry about Charles's grandfather.

Sonya's voice broke into her thoughts. "Cassie, dear. Are you finished? Why don't we check out the boutiques this morning? Then go to that Ship Shape program. With all this food, we have to keep trim, you know."

Cassie met Sonya's blue gaze. How could she think of shopping and exercising when Charles had just learned of his grandfather's death? His grandfather, whom he was to meet for the very first time. "No thanks, Sonya. You and Lisa go. I'm going to see Charles. He's all alone."

"But, Cassie, his cousin is boarding ship tomorrow. He'll be a great comfort to Charles."

"He's not here now. Anyway, Charles doesn't even know his cousin."

Sonya's pink mouth tightened, little lines furrowing above her upper lip. "It's up to you, of course. I just thought a little fun might lighten up the atmosphere." She opened her compact, checked her lipstick, and snapped the compact shut. "Maybe we ladies can shop tomorrow in Puerto Rico while your father goes to his meeting. Don't you think that would be a good idea, James?"

James sipped his coffee. "Certainly. That would be fine if you want to shop tomorrow." He placed the folded newspaper on the table and stood up. "See you all at lunch. I've quite a bit of work to do now."

"And after lunch we play cards," said Lisa.

"Right, Lisa. Maybe Cassie and Charles will join us." He shot a look at Cassie and left.

He's always leaving, thought Cassie.

Lisa drained her glass, leaving a milk mustache.

"Maybe Cassie doesn't want to go shopping with us," she said.

Sonya smiled. "We'd have a wonderful time. And you really could use some new clothes, Cassie."

Cassie bristled. She and her mother had shopped together for this cruise. "I don't need any more clothes," she said, pushing her chair back and standing up. "Excuse me." She left the table, feeling as alone as Charles was.

Still seething from Sonya's remarks, Cassie hurried to Charles's room. Heartless, she thought. That's what Sonya was. She didn't care at all about Charles. And her father. He didn't care about her. Just his work and his new family. I wish I hadn't come. But then, there's Charles. He needs a friend. He has no one.

Cassie rapped on Charles's door. Let him be here. I've got to talk to him.

Charles opened the door. He was holding a worn piece of paper in his hand. Color flushed his cheeks. "Come on in," he said, stepping back.

Cassie couldn't help noticing how neat the room was. Nothing like Lisa's and mine, she thought. "Are you all right, Charles?" she asked.

"Sure. I'm all right," he said, his voice breaking. He turned away abruptly.

Cassie felt she had barged in. Maybe Charles would rather be alone. She watched him place the paper on his desk and smooth it out. To break the silence, she asked, "What's that?"

He looked at the paper. "It's a letter I got from my grandfather. It's why I'm on this trip."

Cassie shifted her weight from one foot to the other. Curiosity piqued, she asked, "What's it about?"

"You wouldn't understand it unless I told you about my family first," he said, darting a quick glance at her.

Cassie sensed his discomfort. Pulling out the desk chair to sit down, she said, "Well, if you've got family problems, you're not the only one. You know the situation I'm in."

Charles grinned. "Sonya's something else." He sat on the edge of his bed, fingering the ring he wore around his neck. "The ring is part of the story." He hesitated, then, seeming to make up his mind, told Cassie his family history.

"My father was vacationing in Martinique when he met my mother. They fell in love, and she ran away with him. My grandfather was furious. When I was younger, I'd ask my mother about her life on Martinique. She used to describe the mountains, the beaches, and the family plantation. But she never talked about her father. If I asked about him, she'd get very quiet and sad." Charles paused and clasped his hands together. "From the little she did say, I think they were once very close. He didn't get married until he was older. He was forty when my mother was born, and she was an only child. Her mother died when she was a baby."

Charles stood up and gazed out the porthole. "So you see, I don't know how I feel about my grandfather's death. He didn't treat my mother very well. And, anyway, I never knew him, never even met him, but . . ."

"But you wanted to meet him, and . . . he was a link with your mom. Right?" Cassie prompted.

Charles nodded. "When I was twelve, my father told me to stop pestering my mother with questions about her past. That she was an American citizen now, with a family of her own."

Cassie heard the sorrow in Charles's voice. She stood, wanting to give him a hug, but felt shy. He turned and handed her the well-read paper.

Cassie looked up from the black letters that sprawled over the paper. "Charles, I can't read this. It's not in English."

"Oh, sorry," said Charles, taking the letter back. "I'll read it to you. I know it by heart, in French and English."

Charles's voice broke a little as he read the letter. As Cassie listened, she sank back into the chair, eyes wide, mouth slightly open.

To my dear grandson, Charles,

On learning of your mother's death—my own dear daughter—I realized how foolish the rift between us has been. If only we could go back in time—but, alas, we cannot—I would make it up to her.

As she may have told you, after she ran away to marry your father, I told her never to come back. The foolish words of a hurt and adoring father.

Needless to say, I regretted my words as soon as I spoke them, but such words—once uttered—cannot be taken back. They hang in the air like sharp needles—between people, prickling, hurting.

A few years ago, I sent her a ring as a token—an apology. A garnet with a lion's image. Rather large for a woman, but it had been mine, and I wanted her to have it. Perhaps she showed it to you?

My dear grandson, one rift leads to others, and because of my angry words so many years ago, I have been denied the pleasure of knowing you. I grow older, and the doctors say my heart is bad. Before the end of my time, I would like to meet my only grandson and share with him a family secret—a secret that our family has borne for nearly a century. And perhaps he, as the youngest member of the Nobre family, can put it to rights.

I know this—my first letter to you—is a strange one. Ask your father, nay, plead with him, to let you come to visit the Nobre Plantation and ease an old man's grief. As a token of the coming reconciliation between our estranged families, wear the garnet ring I sent your mother—my dear daughter. It would please me greatly.

Your loving grandfather,

Jerome Nobre

Cassie sprang to her feet. "A secret. And he wants you to 'put it to rights.' Charles, do you suppose . . . do you think it could be. . ."—her voice sank to a whisper—"the Jeweled Jesu?"

Charles shook his head. "No way."

Cassie chewed on her lower lip, and her eyes

squinted with concentration, said, "Doesn't that letter say something about the secret being nearly a century old? And I remember you asked Professor Ornard yesterday when Mount Pelée erupted. Nineteen hundred and two, right? A century ago. That's how long the Jeweled Jesu's been missing, and the secret's just as old."

Charles shrugged. "That's a crazy idea, Cassie."

Cassie couldn't understand his denial. "Did your mother ever mention a secret?" she asked.

"No . . ." Charles's voice was hesitant. He stood very still, but Cassie could feel tension radiating from him. "She did say that my grandfather and great-uncle disagreed about something. Sometimes, they had terrible fights."

"Your great-uncle?"

Charles nodded. "My grandfather's brother, Claude. My cousin Jacques's father."

"What did they fight about—your grandfather and great-uncle?"

Charles looked at Cassie, then away. "Once, she heard them shouting about a . . . a statue," he mumbled.

Excitement bubbled through Cassie. "A statue! You see, Charles?"

Charles struck the desk with the palm of his hand. "Cassie, listen to me. I don't want it to be the Jeweled Jesu. Remember what Professor Ornard said about the statue? Whoever has it will suffer misfortune, and the family too—forever and ever."

Cassie, startled, shrank back. "But, that's just superstition."

"Is it? How come my mother died so young? How come her father disowned her?" Charles's dark eyes flashed. "And how would you feel, Cassie, if someone in your family had taken the Jeweled Jesu and hidden it away?" He rushed on, not waiting for an answer. "Like a thief, that's how."

Cassie saw the hurt in Charles's eyes. How insensitive she'd been. Thinking of the missing Jeweled Jesu as an exciting mystery. How would she feel in his place? She knew that neither her father nor mother would keep something that belonged to someone else. But what about a grandparent or a great-grandparent? She couldn't know that.

Cassie's arms spread wide. Fervently, she said, "But Charles, your grandfather wanted to tell you the secret. And, he wanted you"—she pointed to the letter with a trembling finger—" 'as the youngest member of the Nobre family' to make things right. And, anyway, Charles, it's not your fault."

Charles pushed a hand through his dark hair and straightened his shoulders. "You're right, Cassie. It's not my fault." He took a deep breath. "And maybe I can do something about it. Maybe, if the secret is the Jeweled Jesu, I can find it and return it to the church."

Cassie clasped her hands and said softly, "That would make your grandfather and your mother proud." Her eyes widened. "Oh, I wish I could help you."

Charles put his hands on her shoulders, and they gazed into each other's eyes. Cassie saw something new in his eyes, and her heart skipped a beat.

His voice cracked a little when he said, "Do you think your parents—I mean, your father and Sonya—would let you come to the plantation?"

Cassie flushed and smiled. "Oh, I'd love that! We could search for the Jeweled Jesu, and I could get away from Sonya and Lisa for a while."

"If it is the Jeweled Jesu," Charles cautioned. "Anyway, ask your father today," he urged. "We get to Martinique Thursday morning, and the ship docks there till Saturday. You could spend that time at the plantation."

Cassie frowned. "What about your cousin and your great-uncle? Maybe they wouldn't want a visitor. After all, your grandfather . . ."

"I know. I was just thinking about that." Charles paced a few steps in the small room. "I meet my cousin Jacques tomorrow. I'll ask him then. We'll work something out."

"What's your cousin Jacques like?" asked Cassie.

Charles shrugged. "My mother never said much about him—except that he was a spoiled only son. He was a lot younger than she was."

Cassie pointed to the ring that hung around Charles's neck. "The ring, Charles. Do you think there's a connection?"

"I was wondering the same thing. But I've checked and checked it. There's no inscription—just a lion's image on the stone." Charles removed the ring and handed it to Cassie.

Studying the ring, she said, "I almost forgot to tell you. Professor Ornard said he'd look at our rings today."

Charles cocked his head toward the door, then put his fingers to his lips. "I think I hear someone," he whispered. He tiptoed to the door and pulled it open.

Larson stood there, fumbling with the keys that hung from his belt.

Charles scowled. "What do you want? The room's all made up."

Indicating a pile of towels draped over his left

forearm, Larson said, "Just bringing some fresh towels. I ran out before." He brushed by Charles and into the bathroom.

Cassie and Charles stood watching him. When he stepped back into the cabin, his bulk seemed to fill the room.

Rocking on the balls of his feet, he grinned. "What are you two doing in this stuffy cabin?" he asked.

Cassie's face burned at his insinuating tone and at the way he was looking at her. She glanced at Charles and saw his olive cheeks darken.

Larson folded his arms across his chest and leaned against the door jamb. "There's lots to do out on deck, you know." Flexing his arms, he said, "You don't get muscles like these staying indoors. You ever try any sports, Charlie?"

"Basketball. And the name's Charles," Charles said shortly.

"Basketball—um. I'm an outdoors man myself. Snorkeling. Now that's a great sport." His eyes fell to the ring swinging from the chain looped over Cassie's hand. "Pretty ring. Is it yours?"

Cassie slipped the chain over her neck. Ignoring his question, she said, "Snorkeling? I've always wanted to try that."

Sliding his eyes up and down her body, Larson grinned and said, "You look to be in pretty good shape, but you also have to be a good swimmer to snorkel."

Cassie, flustered, said, "I am a good swimmer."

Leaning toward her, he said, "Then sign up for my snorkeling group when we get to Little Martinique. You'll be safe with me. I've won medals swimming, you know."

Charles, a deep scowl on his brow, said rudely, "Thanks for the towels."

"Right," said Larson with a mock salute. He winked at Cassie and left, shutting the door behind him.

Cassie, her heart thumping, stared at the door. Larson's attention was both unsettling and flattering. When Charles had taken her by the shoulders and looked into her eyes, she'd felt warm and happy, but Larson . . . she wasn't sure how he'd made her feel.

Fingering the ring, she wondered why she had let him think it was hers. It had been an instinctive reaction. But why?

"Do you like that guy?" asked Charles. He sat on the edge of his bed, frowning.

Cassie stammered. "I . . . I don't know. He's all right, I guess."

"I don't like him. And, if I were you, I'd be careful. I wouldn't trust him."

Cassie bridled. Charles sounded jealous and bossy. He had no right to tell her what or what not to do.

"He's older, too. Twenty. He's been around a lot."

"How do you know that?" asked Cassie.

"He told me. He bragged all about his swimming medals. Said he had hopes for the Olympics, but something happened in his senior year. I'm not sure what. He dropped out of school, and now he's just drifting around from job to job. He signed on to this ship to help with the sports program. Then, at the last minute, one of the stewards got sick, so he's filling in for him, too. Anyway," he said curtly, "what do you think of the ring?"

Ignoring his brusque tone, Cassie lifted the chain over her head. She pressed the stone with her forefinger. "The stone's a little loose. I like the engraving. Are you going to take it to the professor today?"

Charles, seeming to forget about Larson, said, "Definitely. He might, at least, be able to tell me what the lion stands for. I'll catch him before his lecture."

"I'll meet you there. I want to ask him about my ring, too."

"Okay. And don't forget: Ask your father about Martinique."

Cassie laughed. "Forget? No chance." Humming a little tune, Cassie hurried down the hall. Turning a corner, she bumped into Enrico. Averting his eyes, he ignored her greeting. It wasn't until sometime later she wondered why a busboy was in the passenger quarters.

Chapter 5

Cassie studied the book display in the Logo Shop. After she left Charles's room, a nagging sense of guilt had driven her to the boutiques to look for Sonya and Lisa. She knew she hadn't been living up to the promise she had made to her mother before the trip—the promise to try her best to get along with her father's new wife and stepdaughter.

She couldn't help but contrast Charles's family situation with her own. His mother and grandfather, both dead, and his father—always away on business trips. At least her father had asked her on this cruise. She would try harder. She would.

She had checked all the shops but found no sign of Sonya or Lisa. She glanced at her watch. Maybe they were at that exercise class?

A pile of Professor Ornard's books caught her eye. She studied the picture of the Jeweled Jesu on the cover of *Gemstones—Their Mystical Power and Symbolism*. Her breath quickened. What if . . . ? She picked up a copy of each book and took them to the center counter. Waiting in line to pay for them, she saw Sonya and Lisa.

They were rummaging through a pile of sweat-shirts. Sonya pulled out a hot pink one and held it against Lisa.

Cassie heard the salesgirl say, "Lovely color on her."

Sonya's bright smile. "Isn't it? She has such a lovely complexion."

"Oh, Mom," Lisa said. But she took the shirt from her mother and, holding it against her chest, studied herself in a narrow mirror.

Cassie saw the pleased smile on her face, and suddenly realized Lisa was actually pretty when she smiled. Suddenly Cassie felt shy and awkward, not sure she'd be welcome if she joined them. She paid for the books and left.

Deciding to take the books to a quiet, shady spot she liked on the sports deck six levels up, she pushed the elevator button. The doors screeched open; two women got out, and Cassie stepped in to find herself face-to-face with her father.

A frown creased his brow, and his heavy briefcase seemed to weigh him down. His eyes dropped to the books Cassie carried. "I see you bought the professor's books." The elevator stopped; and the doors slid open to the commodore deck, where his and Sonya's stateroom was. "Step out here with me, Cassie. I want to talk to you."

A command. Why did he always sound like a commander in chief? Her mother used to say it was because of his work. He gave orders and others obeyed. And he couldn't leave work behind, couldn't relax. Well, he was on a cruise. What better place to relax? Maybe he would after his big meeting in Puerto Rico tomorrow.

They sat on one of the benches in the small lobby. It was quiet here—away from the activity decks. Only the view of endless water from the window and the slight rocking motion told Cassie she was on a ship.

Now, she thought, is the time to ask him about going to the plantation. But she hesitated, not knowing how to start, not knowing how to talk to this man who was her father.

It seemed a million years ago that she had sat on

his lap and he had ruffled her hair and called her "Cassie Lassie." Questions flashed through her mind. Why? Why did you leave Mom, Danny, and me? Why did you want a new family? What was the matter with ours?

James Hartt cleared his throat. "Are you enjoying the cruise, Cassie?" he asked.

Cassie glanced at her father's face, then stared straight ahead. "Mm," she answered. Then, summoning courage, she said, "I was just talking to Charles. He was so upset about his grandfather's death. He's really all alone, you know. He asked me if I could visit his relatives' plantation while we're in Martinique."

"Cassie, I'm sorry for Charles and his family situation, but you're here to visit me . . . and Sonya and Lisa."

"But . . ." Cassie traced the picture of the silver and jeweled statue on the book cover.

Her father pulled his half-glasses out of his shirt pocket and slipped them on. He took the book from her and studied the cover. "Beautiful," he murmured. "Is this the Jeweled Jesu you were talking about?"

Cassie nodded. What could she say to convince him to let her go?

Returning the book to her, he said, "So you did

go shopping after all. That was nice of you. Must have pleased Sonya."

Cassie, too edgy to sit, stood up. "I did go shopping, but not with Sonya and Lisa. I decided to. Then, when I saw them, I thought . . . well, I mean, I thought maybe they really wouldn't want me there—"

James Hartt interrupted. "Cassie, of course they wanted you. Didn't Sonya ask you several times this morning? Stop making excuses."

Stung, Cassie remained silent. Her father would never understand.

James Hartt pulled gently on Cassie's elbow, urging her to sit down. "Look, Cassie. I was hoping you would become friends with Sonya and Lisa on this trip. You know, you'd like them if you'd give them half a chance."

Cassie's mouth opened in surprise. "Me give them half a chance? What about Lisa? She'll hardly talk to me."

"She's younger than you, Cassie. And she's had a hard time. Her father deserted them when she was five—"

Cassie interrupted. "And Sonya. All she does is talk about clothes and what color they are. How could you leave Mom for her?"

"Cassie." Her father's voice was sharp. "Don't get

into things you know nothing about. I didn't just leave your mother. It was something we both wanted. What I want to talk to you about now is this trip. I want you to make more of an effort. When your mother suggested you come with us, I—"

Cassie sprang to her feet. Her voice tight, she said, "What do you mean 'your mother suggested'? I thought it was your idea."

James Hartt looked into his daughter's eyes, then, sighing, looked away. "We both thought it was a good idea."

"But Mom suggested it first?" Cassie insisted. How could her mother do such a thing to her? And she had let Cassie think it was her father's idea.

James Hartt stood and placed his hands on Cassie's shoulders. "What does it matter who suggested it first? I wanted you here with us. I'm your father and—"

Cassie's ears were ringing, and her head ached. She clenched the books against her chest. Words flooded from her as though on the crest of a wave. "You're not my father anymore. Not really."

Her father's lips tightened into a straight line. "Of course, I'm your father. I'll always be your father."

Cassie, swallowing against the tightness in her throat, shook herself free and ran to the staircase.

Chapter 6

Cassie raced to the sun walk on the compass deck. Few passengers ventured here, and she welcomed the solitude. She tossed her books on one of the lounge chairs and paced back and forth along the railing.

It had been her mother's idea that she go on this cruise, not her father's. Why? She had never said anything to her mother about her feelings after the divorce. She had pretended, even to herself, that everything was fine, that she didn't miss her father. Then, when the opportunity for this trip came along, the chance to spend time with him—time, not just a weekend phone call—she had let the hope grow that her father did care, that he really loved her. What a fool she was. A stupid fool. She had been foisted on him.

Cassie retreated from the sun and wind to an oasis of shade. She kicked the chair, then sat down, pulling her hair from her hot, sticky face. She picked up the books and swung her legs onto the lounge chair. Taking a deep breath, she willed her heart to stop racing. She had other things to think about. And the trip would soon be over. He'd be rid of her, and she'd never have to see him again.

The Jeweled Jesu glowed on the book's cover. It had been missing for a century. Where was it? Was it still in one piece?

She just had to go to the plantation with Charles. She could help him find the statue, and she could get away from her father and his family.

She forced thoughts of her father from her mind and began to read, first about gemstones and their mystical power, then the story of Maiden Hill. She read and reread the story, each time identifying more with the young maiden. How awful. Happily watching her future husband play a game, dreaming of their life together, then suddenly savages attacking, killing. Cassie shuddered. Whatever happened to the girl? Why hadn't they found her body? She read right through lunch, ignoring the hunger pangs that gnawed at her belly.

Apparitions—ghosts. Did she believe in them? She thought of the professor and his ankh. He believed. She was sure of it.

The cruise liner moved through the sea. A rope slapped rhythmically against a railing. The sun moved, and Cassie, no longer in a shady oasis, slept, her book opened on her chest.

The murmur of voices came and went as Cassie struggled to stay asleep. The voices grew louder, pulling her to wakefulness. Her skin prickled and itched with sunburn. The scattered lounge chairs were empty except for one, where an elderly man snored gently.

Cassie rubbed the side of her face, felt the imprint of the chair. A name—Nobre—crystallized from the murmured words. Cassie froze, and strained to hear.

The two men were partially behind a funnel. Cassie could see only part of a garish purple-and-red shirt. Professor Ornard. Voice rising, his next words hung in the air: "I tell you, the Nobre boy has something that tells where the treasure is hidden. If it's not the ring, which I'll have in my hands this afternoon, you'll have to search again. The secret lies with him. I know it."

Cassie lay still, not daring to breathe, every muscle tense. Footsteps. Elevator door opening, closing. Silence. The professor's words rang in her head. She and Charles were right. The ring was a clue. But how did the professor fit in? How did he know Charles had a clue to the treasure? And what was the treasure? The Jeweled Jesu?

The Nobre name. She remembered how yesterday, when Charles had given his name as Charles Reyes, the professor had practically dismissed them. But this morning, after he learned that Charles was a Nobre, he had offered to look at his ring.

The ring. Cassie jumped to her feet, and the books fell with a thump. She scooped them up. She had to get to Charles before he gave the professor the ring. She glanced at her watch. Almost time for the professor's lecture.

Cassie raced down the five flights of stairs to the promenade deck. She just knew that if Professor Ornard got Charles's ring in his hands, he'd make some excuse to keep it, examine it, unlock its secret.

She dodged around the sunbathers' chairs and raced into the dimly lit Rainbow Lounge. Air-conditioned air struck her hot skin like a glass of cold water. People were settling into chairs. Blood drumming in her ears, eyes adjusting to the dim light, Cassie searched frantically for Charles. Then she saw them at the far end of the book-stacked table. Charles was lifting the chain with the ring on it from around his neck. The professor's hand curved toward it.

Cassie, clutching her books to her chest, hurried toward them. "Professor," she said eagerly, thrusting the books into his outstretched hands, "I got these in the bookstore. Would you autograph them for me?"

The professor caught the books and glared at Cassie. Smoothly, he said, "Of course. I'll be delighted to autograph the books. But first, I'll take a look at Charles's ring."

He placed the books on the table and swept the ring from Charles's hand. Tracing the image of the lion with a fingernail, he murmured in a singsong voice, "A lion's image engraved on a garnet will protect and preserve the wearer's honor and health, cure him of all diseases, bring him honor, and guard him from all dangers in traveling."

Cassie recognized the words she had just read in the gemology book. Holding her breath, she watched the professor turn the ring around with the tips of his fingers, then, with a long nail, press the stone.

Stretching his face into a smile, he said to Charles, "The stone's loose. I can fix it for you. Just leave it with me for a bit." He moved to slide the ring and chain into his shirt pocket.

Cassie, who had been struggling to force her tight emerald off her finger, said, "My emerald. You promised to tell me about my ring." The ring came over her reddened knuckle, and she jabbed it into his hand, knocking Charles's ring to the floor, where it fell with a clatter. Both she and the professor bent to retrieve it.

The ring on its gold chain lay near Cassie's foot. She scooped it up. No stone. Cassie scanned the floor for the missing garnet.

The professor held out his hand. "Here. I'll take that. I said I'd fix it for Charles."

Cassie clutched the ring and, on hands and knees, searched for the garnet.

Charles knelt to help her.

A tall, thin woman who had been looking at the books picked one up. "Professor, I'd like this book, please. And would you autograph it?"

Cassie spotted the rich red stone on the other side of the table. She dashed over to it and jammed it and the ring deep into her pocket.

She looked up to see the professor studying her from under hooded eyes as he gave the woman her change. "Ah. You found it. I told you the stone was loose. Now give it to me." He stuck out his hand.

Cassie plucked her emerald from the table and gathered up her books. "We won't bother you with these things now." She smiled brightly. "It's time for your lecture."

She felt the professor's malevolent gaze following her as she and Charles hurried from the room.

Cassie flew to the outside deck, her heart pounding with excitement. At the railing, she whirled and faced Charles, who regarded her with raised eyebrows. "What was that all about?" he asked.

"Charles. The ring." She pulled the setting and stone from her pocket and held them out on her open palm to Charles. Sunlight lit the garnet, brightened the gold. "The secret's in the ring," she breathed. "Upstairs, on the compass deck, I heard the professor talking to someone. He wants your ring. He knows there's a connection between the ring and 'the treasure.' That's what he said. And I bet the treasure is the Jeweled Jesu."

Cassie peered at the setting. "See this gold base. I was just reading that most rings don't have gold under the stone. It blocks the light. I bet it's a false bottom."

Charles took the ring from Cassie and examined it closely. "The plate has lines in it. Maybe it opens." He drew a jackknife from his pocket and inserted its thin blade into the outer-most line of the base. Gently prodding, he lifted the thin plate of gold. His shoulders sagged. "Nothing," he said. "There's nothing in here."

"There's got to be," said Cassie, taking the ring from his hand. "There's not even room for a piece of paper," she murmured, her voice heavy with disappointment.

Charles was rubbing the minute panel of gold between his thumb and fingers. "This feels kind of rough," he said, holding it to the light. "Let's see if they have a magnifying glass at the Logo Shop, then take this to my room for a look."

In his room, Charles studied the engraving on the backside of the panel with the magnifying glass. "It looks like two letters," he murmured. "M and H. And three circles. A small one. A large one. Then a real tiny one with an X in it."

"Let me see," said Cassie, reaching for the glass and thin gold plate. Peering at the tiny letters, she murmured, "M. H. M. H." Wide-eyed, she stared at Charles and whispered, "Maiden's Hill. I bet that's it." A shiver crept down her spine. "Maiden's Hill. That's where the Jeweled Jesu is."

Charles, his dusky cheeks flushed and his dark eyes almost black, grasped her shoulders and looked into her eyes. "Cassie, you've got to stay at the plantation with me."

Cassie's face fell. "I asked my father. I ran into him after I left you this morning."

"He said no?" Charles said.

"Yes—and then he started lecturing me. I ran away from him." She couldn't tell Charles how her mother had forced her father to ask her to go on the cruise. It was too humiliating. All this time she had thought her father wanted her there.

Charles narrowed his eyes and ran his hand through his hair. "We've got to persuade him. Maybe Sonya would help."

Cassie's eyes widened. "Sonya?"

"Mm. Maybe you could work on her."

"I don't know. We're not very chummy."

"We've got to think of something," said Charles. He took the plate from her hand and trained the magnifying glass on it. "What do you suppose these circles mean?" he asked. "Three of them. A small one. A larger one. Then this tiny one with an X in it. Well," he murmured, "X marks the spot, so they say."

Cassie squinted at the gold plate. "But what spot?" she mused.

Chapter 7

Shore Excursion

San Juan, Puerto Rico.
Population: 1,086,400.
Language: Spanish is the official language, but almost everyone speaks English, too.
Climate: The average temperature is 77 degrees Fahrenheit.
Currency: The U.S. dollar.
Arrive: 8:00 A.M.
Depart: 6:00 P.M.
For group tours, apply to the cruise director's office, or enjoy the day browsing and shopping at leisure.

A blast of the ship's horn vibrated through Cassie's feet. She shook Charles's arm. "You've got the ring, right?" she asked.

Charles chuckled. "Cassie, you know I do."

Cassie waited impatiently to disembark. Today, in San Juan, she and Charles hoped to crack the ring's secret. In the bibliography of the professor's book on superstitions, he had listed *Exploring the Caves of the Caribbean,* published by the Caribbean National Museum, San Juan, Puerto Rico. Today, they planned to find that book.

Cassie leaned forward to watch as a crack in the ship's side opened, then creaked slowly down to form a platform. A blast of warm, salty air blew in, lifting her hair. She stretched forward for a glimpse of the tender that would ferry them to San Juan. It bobbed about in small whitecaps whipped by the wind. Members of the crew, smart in their white jackets and navy slacks, assisted the passengers from the ship to the runway. Cassie hung on to the chain railing, then stepped into the rocking tender. She and Charles sat behind her father, Sonya, and Lisa. Dad looks out of place in that business suit, she thought.

Last night after dinner, he had pulled her aside.

"Cassie, we've got to talk, get things straightened out. It's hard after all this time . . ." He had run his hands through his thinning hair. "You know, I keep thinking of you as a little girl. In the past year, you've grown so much, and . . ."

Cassie had noticed the tired lines around his eyes. She had wanted to reach out to him—be his little girl again, feel secure in his love. But he had left them. He had a new family. And she was here only because her mother had suggested it.

Charles nudged an elbow into her ribs. "Here comes the professor," he whispered.

"Good morning, everyone. This mode of transportation is a bit smaller than the one we just left. Quite a difference, eh?" He stood at an angle facing them, his legs planted firmly apart to keep his balance, tufts of black hair poking through his yellow mesh shirt.

Sonya, unusually quiet, smiled a half-smile. "I'll certainly be glad to get on land, Professor," she said. Cassie noted the greenish tinge around her mouth.

Philippe Ornard slipped into the seat next to Charles. "On the big ship, you hardly feel the motion. Out here, you appreciate the sea's power. So . . . young Charles, today you meet your cousin. Is that not so?"

"Tonight," Charles said. "I'll meet him on board ship tonight."

"Tonight? So, you won't be spending the day with him?"

"No," Charles answered.

The professor slid his eyes toward Cassie, then back to Charles. "It's too bad the stone fell out of your ring yesterday, Charles. Bring it to me tomorrow and I'll fix it for you."

Sonya, struggling to keep her pink straw hat from blowing away, turned and, smiling valiantly, said, "You know, Professor, you've really kindled an interest in ghosts and caves and all that scary stuff in the children. Lisa was telling me that Cassie and Charles are off to museums today to see what they can find out about Caribbean caves."

Lisa, snapping her gum, stared at the professor.

"Maybe Lisa would like to go with Cassie and Charles," said Cassie's father, shrugging off his lightweight suit jacket.

The professor, absently rubbing his ring, beads of perspiration on his long upper lip, turned his hooded gaze to Charles. "Off to museums, eh? Which ones are you going to?"

Cassie leaned across Charles, blocking him from the professor, and tapped Lisa on the shoulder. "Do you want to come with us, Lisa?"

Lisa stopped chewing her gum and, wide-eyed, considered Cassie's question. She shifted in her chair and looked away. "No, I'm going shopping with Mom," she said.

Cassie was relieved that Lisa had said no. She had only asked to interrupt the professor, of course. But her father's look of gratitude pleased her.

The tender was pulling into dock, and people surged forward, jamming the exit way. Charles and Cassie stepped past the professor and joined the crowd, welcoming the noise and confusion to escape him.

They wove through traffic blocking the dock area and entered a narrow street. "Look," cried Charles, "isn't that Enrico, the busboy?"

Cassie glimpsed Enrico disappearing up a side street. "He's probably visiting someone here. Did you know his wife's expecting their seventh baby? Fernando says that's why Enrico's inattentive sometimes. He's worried about his family. I guess he doesn't make much money as a busboy. I nearly fell over him yesterday when I left your room."

Charles frowned. "I wonder what he was doing down there. Busboys and waiters aren't supposed to go to passenger quarters."

Cassie shrugged. "Do you have that city map?" she asked. "I think we've got quite a walk to the museum, then we've got to find a jeweler to set the stone and get back in time to meet Sonya and Lisa for lunch."

"Too bad about the lunch. If we didn't have to meet them, we'd have a lot more time," said Charles, opening up the map.

"I know." Cassie sighed. "But it was the only way my father would agree to our going off alone."

They squeezed against a building at an intersection and studied the map. "Straight up five blocks, then left on Calle San Sebastian. We'll have to keep track of these street names," Cassie said, wiping beads of perspiration from her forehead.

They continued up the steadily climbing streets, the traffic and crowds gradually lessening. Turning onto yet another street, Cassie stopped as an eerie feeling spread over her. She slowed her pace and said to Charles, "Someone's following us. Don't turn," she warned as his head swiveled round.

"Cassie, your imagination is running wild. No one's following us. Come on, the museum should be on the next street."

"Charles." Cassie pulled on his arm. "You should give me the ring. If someone is following us, they'd expect you to have it."

"You're serious," said Charles. "Okay. When we get to the museum, I'll give it to you."

"Where is the ring?"

"Right here." He patted his left breast pocket. "But I have the panel in my other pocket. I'm not going to have it put back in the ring. That way we can study it whenever we want to."

"Be careful you don't lose it," Cassie cautioned. "It's so small."

They climbed white stone steps to the museum and entered its enormous central patio. "This place is so big," said Cassie, looking at the people wandering through arched doors that led to spacious galleries. "How will we find anything?"

"Over there," said Charles, steering her toward the information booth in the center of the room. A slim, dark-haired girl at the desk explained how to get to the gift shop. "If we have that book, it would be there," she told them in accented English.

In the second-floor shop, Cassie nudged Charles. "The ring," she said, holding out her hand.

Charles nodded, gave her the setting and stone, and watched as she tucked the two pieces into the zippered pouch she wore around her waist.

They found *Exploring the Caves of the Caribbean.* The book gave the location approximate depth and size of each cave. A drawing symbolized the number of passages and rooms. Under Martinique, they found Maiden's Hill. Cassie turned to it with trembling fingers. "It's got to have the same diagram as the gold panel," she murmured. "Here it is."

She spread the book on a counter, and she and Charles looked at it, then at each other, puzzled frowns on their faces. "Only two rooms," said Charles.

"But it's shaped just like your grandfather's diagram. Except for that extra space with the X in it," said Cassie.

"Cassie, is that Larson over there?"

She scanned the room. "Where?"

But Charles was already out the door. Cassie caught up to him, where he stood, hands on hips, surveying the arches to several galleries. A Spanish-speaking tour guide gestured to a chattering group to gather around him.

Cassie, catching her breath, said, "What would Larson be doing in a museum? He doesn't seem the type. It must have been someone who looks like him."

Charles said, "You thought someone was following us, remember?"

Uneasiness tugged at Cassie. Larson. He had asked about the ring. Had he searched Charles's room? Had he followed them? She tried to ignore the sense of disquiet growing in her. "Let's buy the book, then get your ring fixed," she said brusquely.

Traffic rumbled down the narrow street. Tourists and natives jostled one another. A heavyset man, arms swinging wide, lumbered past Cassie, causing her to lose her balance and stumble into the street. She felt the heat of the cars, smelled the oily fumes of diesel fuel. A horn shrilled.

Cassie hopped back onto the narrow walk. Where was Charles? She hurried to where he stood studying the street map. "What a mob! Some man knocked me into the street," she complained.

Charles looked up from the map. "Who knocked you into the street?" he asked, frowning.

"Just some big guy," said Cassie, peering over his shoulder at the map. "Where to next?" she asked.

"There're some jewelry stores on Calle San Francisco. How much time do we have?"

Cassie eyed her watch. "Plenty. And, from the looks of the map, we're working our way back to the pier."

They made their way from store to store. Two jewelers turned them away. Too busy, they said. Leave the ring. Come back tomorrow. Now, the third jeweler handed the stone and setting back to Cassie. She looked at them lying in the palm of her hand, thinking of Charles's grandfather, so many years ago, marking the secret panel with intricate detail. But what did that third circle and X mean? Why hadn't a third passage been indicated in the book? A woman holding a baby shoved by her. Cassie thrust her hand into her shorts pocket. Back on the street, feeling uneasy, she glanced over her shoulder.

"Do you still think someone's following us?" Charles asked.

Cassie, trying to convince herself, shook her head. "Couldn't be. We made sure no one was around when we left the museum. Anyway, it's broad daylight. What could happen?"

Charles pursed his lips and raised an eyebrow. "We don't really have to get the ring fixed, you know."

"But the professor would bug you about it."

"I could just tell him it was fixed."

"He'd want to see it."

"But I'm keeping the panel out; he could just set the stone."

"He could tell something was missing. Right now he can't be sure there's a clue in the ring."

They had been weaving their way through the crowded street, separated occasionally as they stepped around people who were window-shopping.

The unrelenting heat, the smell of exhaust fumes, and the noise of impatient horns made Cassie dizzy.

Across the street, she spied another jewelry store. "Let's try that one," she yelled above the racket. "Come on. The traffic's stopped. We can cross here."

"Cassie, wait," called Charles, bending to retrieve the map that had fallen from his pocket.

But Cassie was already maneuvering through the stopped traffic to the other side of the street. The light at the corner turned, and engines growled. A huge truck shifted gears. Cassie waved to Charles, who was glaring at her. "Go cross at the light. I'll meet you in the store," she shouted.

She started toward the jewelry store. A group of people sauntered along in front of her. Cassie itched to pass them but didn't want to step back into the teeming street. She hurried by a narrow, dark alleyway.

People flowed out of the next store, crowding the walk even more. Cassie found herself hemmed in, away from the street, pushed against the building. The jewelry store was just past the next alley.

Suddenly, strong hands grabbed her, pulled her into the dark passage. A thick arm crossed her middle, pinning her arms. A meaty hand covered her mouth, stopping her scream.

Cassie's eyes bulged. Every nerve in her body

leaped and shuddered. This couldn't happen. Not in broad daylight, on a crowded street. Struggling against the arms dragging her farther into the alley, she saw, as though in a dream, the people passing by. Automatons. Talking. Laughing.

The hand against her mouth pressed her lips into her teeth. She tasted blood. Felt dizzy. Light-headed. The hand released its pressure. But before Cassie could utter a sound, she was thrust forward. Her head slammed against the brick wall, and she slipped into whirling darkness.

Cassie's head ached. Gingerly, she touched the throbbing lump above her right temple. A fetid odor made her stomach churn.

Charles's voice filtered through a haze. "Cassie. Cassie. Are you all right?" He held her by her shoulders.

Cassie forced her eyes open and looked into Charles's frightened gaze. Above him stood a blurry figure. Groaning, the man lowered his weight and crouched beside her. Cassie, her mind clearing, recognized the blue-and-white uniform of a policeman.

His voice sympathetic, he said, "You'll be all right, miss." Helping her sit up, he nodded toward Charles. "Your boyfriend here couldn't find you. So, he got me. Smart thing to do. Now, tell us what happened?"

Pain shot through Cassie's left hip. Cautiously, she probed her side. Beneath a tear in her shorts, her skin was tender. "My pouch. He ripped my pouch off," she moaned.

"It figures," said the policeman, assisting her to her feet. "Have to watch your belongings, you know. It's too bad, but tourists are easy marks. Come on, I'll take you to the police station, where you can fill out a report. Where can I reach your family?"

Alarmed, Cassie begged, "Oh, please don't bother them. Please. They'll just be upset, and I'm all right. Really I am."

"Sorry, miss. I've got to contact them. Now, where are they?"

Reluctantly, Cassie muttered, "We were supposed to meet them at the Casa Lisboa."

The officer guided her and Charles into a small, stuffy room at the police station. Cassie's knees felt wobbly, and her head ached. Oh, no, they're already here, she thought, spying Sonya and Lisa sitting on a stiff-backed couch.

Sonya sprang from the couch and rushed to Cassie. "Thank heavens you're here. What ever happened to you? Just look at you—your clothes are torn, and your mouth's a mess. I knew you should have come with Lisa and me. We should have stayed together, and this never would have happened." Her icy, pink-nailed hand gripped Cassie's arm, and she led her to the unyielding couch. Lisa stood up and stared at Cassie.

Sonya perched next to her; then, wringing her hands, she jumped to her feet, saying, "I've called your father. He should be here soon."

Her words shot through Cassie's throbbing head. "My father? You called him? But he's at that important meeting—"

"He left the number with me just in case of an emergency." Sonya's hand fluttered to her throat. "Thank heavens. You never know what teenagers are going to get into."

Cassie bit back an angry retort. How unfair. It wasn't her fault she'd been robbed. She pressed her fingertips against her forehead. Her father's meeting. What had he said? He'd been trying to get hold of that man for months. He'd really be angry with her now. First, she'd been foisted on him by her mother. Now this. She stood up and walked to the window, tuning out Sonya's chatter. No breeze stirred through the screened opening to freshen the stale, smoky smelling air. Cassie slid her hands into her pockets. Felt a firm circle, a hard stone. The ring.

The ring! She could hardly believe it. How had it come to be in her pocket? Then she remembered. That woman with the baby had brushed by her, and Cassie had stuffed the ring into her pocket, meaning to transfer it to the pouch later.

A surge of relief flowed through her—they still had the ring. True, Charles had the gold panel, but Cassie felt they were safer if no one knew they had uncovered the ring's secret.

She looked at Charles, who was trying to explain what had happened to Sonya. "Char—" she cried, but the words died in her throat as she saw her father walk in.

Chapter 8

The coastline of Puerto Rico faded, then merged with the sea as Cassie watched from the porthole in her room. She winced as she touched the tender spot on her hip where the pouch buckle had bitten into her flesh.

Her father had insisted she take a nap when they got back to the ship. At first, she hadn't been able to sleep. Every time she closed her eyes, she felt rough hands grabbing her, smelled again the sour smell of garbage. Finally, she had fallen into a heavy sleep, lulled by the gentle rocking of the ship.

She let the drape fall into place and leaned back against the small, firm pillow. Gnawing at her bottom lip, she thought of her father bursting through the door at the police station, harried and upset. Upset, she thought, that his meeting had been interrupted.

Sonya had rushed to him, thrown her arms around him, babbling about how sorry she was to disturb him but she didn't know what to do when the policeman approached her in the restaurant and said Cassie was being brought into the station. . .

Cassie's heart sank. Sonya makes it sound as though I did something wrong, she thought.

Confirming her thoughts, her father asked, "What happened? What did she do? Why was she brought in here?"

The officer at the door said, "She was mugged."

Her father spotted her by the window and, putting Sonya aside, walked briskly to her. Frowning, taking her by the shoulders, he asked, "What happened, Cassie? Are you all right?"

Then Sonya again, clutching his arm, sobbing, "She's all right, James, but what a scare she gave me."

Angry, Cassie turned and punched the hard pillow, grimacing as her weight shifted to her left hip. She shoved the pillow against the wall and tried to get comfortable. She glanced at her watch.

Why hadn't the thief taken that? He had stolen only the pouch. Still, that was the obvious thing to grab. That was where the ring had been. The ring. Had she been right? Had someone been following them? She knew the professor wanted the ring. But . . . would he stalk them? She doubted it. But, maybe . . . he'd send someone else. Enrico? Larson?

Charles was sure he'd seen Larson. Cassie knew Charles didn't like him. Maybe Charles is a little bit jealous, she thought, a smile tugging at her lips.

Lisa came in and flicked on the light. "What are you grinning about?" she asked. "Reliving the adventures of the day?"

Cassie blinked against the sudden brightness. "It wasn't exactly fun, Lisa," she said.

"Mm," said Lisa, rummaging for a bag of potato chips in her bureau drawer. "What some people won't do for attention."

"Knock it off, Lisa. Nobody gets mugged on purpose," Cassie flared.

"Mom said to tell you it's time to get dressed. They wouldn't let me come down here till now. So you could sleep." She sat despondently on the bed, crunching potato chips one by one. "Formal night." She sighed. "Beautiful-people night."

Cassie studied Lisa, who crumpled the chip bag and tossed it at the wastepaper basket, missing but making no move to retrieve it. Her long hair hung heavily around her plump face.

Cassie rubbed her eyes. "That's right. I'd forgotten. And tonight Charles's cousin will be at dinner. I wonder what he's like."

Cassie's spirits lifted at the prospect of dressing up and meeting Charles's cousin. At least it would take her mind off what had happened. If only Lisa weren't such a drag. Looking at the younger girl's morose face, Cassie took a deep breath and said, "Lisa, let's do something different with our hair tonight. After all, as you said, it's beautiful-people night."

Lisa eyed her dubiously. "Like what?" she asked.

"Well," Cassie said, "I could French-braid your hair. It would look great. Your hair's so long and thick, and pulled back from your face, you would look—"

Eyes blazing, Lisa interrupted her. "Would look what?" she snapped. "Thinner. That's what Mom's always saying. I don't want to look thinner. I'm perfectly happy the way I am."

Cassie's eyes widened. "I wasn't going to say thinner, Lisa. I thought it would make you look older." She hesitated, then added, "You're not so heavy, anyway. I bet you lose those extra pounds in a few years."

The cabin soon smelled of steamy showers, powder, and perfume. Cassie studied herself in the dresser mirror, then dabbed makeup at the corner of her mouth to cover the bruise. Her dress was a pale yellow, cocktail length, with thin straps and a scooped neck. Wedging a bobby pin in her upswept hair, she said, "What do you think, Lisa? Will your mother like this color on me?"

At first Lisa had been quiet. But Cassie, determined to make the best of the evening, broke through her gloomy silence when she again offered to do her hair and makeup.

Lisa giggled. "Mom and her colors. I guess she really knows what she's talking about, though." She crowded next to Cassie in front of the small mirror, and her face fell. Sighing, she said, "Mom didn't want me to get this dress. She said it wasn't flattering."

"The color is great, though," Cassie said, laughing. "And a new hairstyle and makeup will do wonders."

Cassie braided Lisa's long, thick hair into a French braid and accented her pale blue eyes with eye shadow and mascara. "You get such a nice tan," she murmured, brushing on a hint of blush.

"I have to be careful or I burn. There," she said, standing back and surveying her artwork. "You look at least thirteen."

Lisa stared at her image. The hairdo made her face look narrower, and the eye shadow deepened the blue of her eyes. She smiled with pleasure.

The girls entered the dining room. Brilliant floral arrangements were centered on each table. Candlelight reflected off glass and silver precisely arranged on pale pink linen.

As they neared their table, Cassie saw Fernando, beaming widely, slide the chair under a newcomer and place a napkin in his lap. Charles's cousin, she thought, curious and excited at the prospect of meeting him.

Fernando's glowing face bathed them in warmth. "Ah, the young ladies. Beautiful. Beautiful." He moved to their places and held their chairs for them.

Charles's cousin stood as they were seated. Cassie glanced quickly at her father, who looked handsome in a white dinner jacket, and smiled at Charles, who looked uncomfortable in a dark gray suit. Both half rose, then resumed their seats.

Cassie glowed under the appreciative look in

Charles's eyes. He introduced his cousin, Jacques Nobre. The man rose again, embarrassing Cassie with his formality. She studied him. Tall, slim, and dark. The family relationship between him and Charles was evident, but he lacked Charles's frank, open look. He wore his white dinner jacket with ease. As he resumed his seat, his eye fell to his lapel, and he flicked at an invisible speck, saying, "It is a pleasure to meet Charles's charming, young friends." He flashed a disarming smile around the table.

Sonya, radiant in metallic pink, preened and smiled back. "It's a pleasure to have you join us, Jacques." Drawing in a deep breath, she said, "Goodness, what a day we've had. You simply wouldn't believe what happened."

Cassie's stomach knotted, and the day's events that she had pushed to the back of her mind washed over her as she listened to Sonya.

"I was so worried when Cassie and Charles didn't show at Casa Lisboa. I knew they wouldn't be late deliberately." She flicked her eyes to Cassie and smiled reassuringly. "I couldn't imagine what had happened. Then, when the police told me they were taking Cassie to the station—why, I wasn't even sure what he was saying; he spoke very broken English, not at all like you, Jacques. Anyway, I just *had* to call my husband. He was at a very important meeting—taking a deposition. I hated to interrupt him, but what else could I do? And at the police station, when they brought Charles and Cassie in! The poor child. She looked so disheveled. She certainly gave me a scare. Teenagers!" She held her hands palms up and raised a shoulder.

James Hartt, frowning, asked Cassie, "Feeling better now?"

His tone was friendly enough, but Cassie thought she detected a hint of impatience in it. She nodded, unconsciously fingering her bruised mouth.

Unobtrusively, Enrico reached for her water glass and filled it. Cassie watched him as he rounded the table. The sight of his thick, strong hands sent a wave of fear through her. She could feel those hands grabbing her, pulling her into the alley. She shuddered. Her imagination was working overtime. Enrico was their busboy, not some thief.

But she and Charles had seen him in San Juan. And she had seen him outside Charles's cabin. Why? Did he know about the ring? Was he working with the professor?

She wanted to see his face, to look him in the eye and determine if he was the one who had robbed her. But, as always, he kept his eyes cast down. Her eyes fell to his thick, square-nailed hands. She tightened into herself, clenching her hands into fists in her lap. Charles, sitting beside her, reached for her hand. He gave it a reassuring squeeze. Cassie looked into his eyes and smiled gratefully. She turned her head and caught Jacques watching her. A flicker of something she didn't like in his eyes, gone as soon as seen, followed by another disarming smile.

Jacques's voice was smooth and consoling. "How terrible for you, Cassie! But the crime rate is horrendous. And, sorry to say, tourists are prime targets. Easy marks, you know. I'd lay a bet that it's a tourist eight times out of ten who gets robbed. I hope you didn't lose anything of great value?"

"Some money and a few odds and ends I had in my waist pouch. The thief didn't even take my watch."

Charles murmured, "And the ring."

"Ring? What ring was that?" asked Jacques sharply.

"The ring Grandfather sent my mother years ago," Charles explained.

"Mm. I remember hearing about that ring. Cassie was carrying it, you say?" he asked, lifting his eyebrows.

Charles nodded. "The stone fell out. We were going to get it fixed at a jeweler's and—"

"No, Charles," said Cassie, laying a hand on his arm. "I haven't had a chance to tell you, but the ring was in my pocket, so it's safe."

Charles looked at her incredulously, then, relief flooding his face, he said, "It was in your pocket? Fantastic! We didn't lose it after all!"

"A bit of lady luck, I'd say," commented Jacques, refilling his wineglass.

James Hartt speared a shrimp. "Is the ring valuable?" he asked.

Again, a nonchalant shrug from Jacques. "I've no idea."

"Better hang on to it, Charles," James advised.

"I'll give it to you later," Cassie said. She glanced at her father, wanting to ask if he'd finished the deposition, but she was afraid to.

Sonya sipped at a glass of grapefruit juice. "Will Charles be staying with you and your father in Martinique? I mean since his grandfather . . ."

Jacques dipped a plump shrimp into spicy cocktail sauce. "Yes, of course, he'll stay with us. But then, he would have been with us, anyway, for we all lived together on the plantation."

"What kind of plantation do you have?" asked James Hartt.

"Rum, sir. Starts out as sugarcane, you know. Acres and acres of sugarcane. We grow it and distill it right there on our own property."

"How exciting!" said Sonya.

Charles and Cassie exchanged a look. Charles, glancing from Jacques to James Hartt, said, "Since the ship will be docked in Martinique for a few days, I was wondering if Cassie could stay at the plantation."

Cassie swallowed, then, her voice higher than she expected, said, "I'd really like to go."

Silence enveloped the table. Cassie thought she saw a flicker of annoyance cross Jacques's face. When she saw her father's mouth clamp into a tight line, she knew he'd say no.

Sonya, her voice bright with enthusiasm, gushed, "What a lovely idea! Such an opportunity for the girls. They'd get to see what life is really like on Martinique, not just visit tourist attractions. I think it's a splendid idea, James. If it's all right with Jacques and his father, I think we should let them go."

Cassie tried to digest what Sonya was saying. "The girls." That meant Lisa. Charles hadn't mentioned Lisa. How could they explore with Lisa there? She'd just get in the way. On the other hand, Sonya's suggestion was a break. Her father might agree for both of them to go, but not her alone. But would Lisa want to go? With these thoughts tumbling through her head, she blurted out, "What do you say, Lisa? We'd get to stay on a real plantation."

Lisa, who was buttering a roll, looked stunned. "I—I don't know," she stumbled.

Charles, responding to Cassie's kick under the table, picked up her cue. "It would be fun, Lisa. We could explore the place. Remember those stories Cassie and I told you about? Haunted caves and ghosts."

Sonya's hands fluttered to her throat. "What are you talking about?"

Clearing his throat, Jacques said, "Charles must be referring to Maiden's Hill. It's supposed to be haunted by a young Arawak girl."

"For heaven's sake. Now don't tell me you believe in ghosts, Jacques," said Sonya.

Jacques smiled and shrugged. "I can only tell you what I hear. Several years ago, a young girl, five or six, was lost in the mountains. They found her on the lower road the next morning. She said a lady with a white light led her to the road." He laughed thinly. "Her mother claimed it must have been the Arawak maiden. The place used to be a great tourist attraction. Of late, few tourists go there. Too far out for them, I imagine. Not far from us, though, Charles. It's a good hike, but you can walk it from the plantation."

He bent his head and, thoughtfully running his thumb over his fingernails, said, "Perhaps it would be a good idea if the girls did join us. Our house is a sad place right now. My father is, of course, grieving for his brother. Ten to one he'd think it's a good idea." He addressed James. "If it's all right with you and your wife, I'm sure my father would welcome guests."

Cassie crossed her fingers under the table and stared at her father intently, willing him to say yes.

He looked from Cassie's to Lisa's expectant faces. "That's very gracious of you, Jacques, but I don't think—"

"Oh, James, let them go. Once you make all those phone calls and set up another appointment for that deposition, we can spend a little time together—alone."

"Well . . ." James hesitated.

"Please, Daddy Jim," Lisa begged.

Cassie swallowed hard, not daring to meet her

father's eyes. He hadn't finished taking the deposition. But now even Lisa was on her side.

"All right. They may go. Providing it's all right with your father, Jacques," he said, his voice terse.

Chapter 9

The garish lights hurt Cassie's eyes, and the clank and clatter of slot machines pounded in her head. Why had she come with Charles and his cousin to the Royal Casino? It had sounded exciting when Jacques had mentioned it at dinner. And certainly better than going to the play with her father, Sonya, and Lisa. But now, her head, which had throbbed through dinner, felt as though it would burst.

She pressed an ice-filled glass of Coke against her temple. She and Charles stood behind the semicircle of stools that flanked the blackjack table. Jacques, perched on one of the stools, slid a chip into the yellow-lined rectangle marked on the red baize. With long, slim fingers, he picked up two more chips and placed them on the first. How much was he betting on this one hand? Those were hundred-dollar chips.

The dealer, a blond woman in a black skirt and a white tuxedo blouse, turned up her last card. Cassie watched as she checked each player's hand and either matched the player's chips or swept them away. She scooped Jacques's away. He palmed his remaining chips and slid from the stool, signaling a waiter for another drink.

He looked as impeccably turned out as he had at the dinner table. But his eyes glowed strangely. Two bright spots of color specked his cheeks, and his mouth was a determined line. He looks like those gamblers in the movies, thought Cassie. And he talks like one, too.

Charles swept a hand through his dark curls. "Too bad you can't memorize all the cards like the guy in a movie I saw."

Something flickered behind Jacques's eyes. Cassie could see that he didn't like Charles's comment. Jacques sure doesn't like to lose, she thought. Looking in his glittering eyes, she shuddered, thinking, I'd hate to have him mad at me.

"The evening has just begun, Charles," Jacques was saying. Nodding toward the blackjack table, he murmured, "This stuff is for tourists. Two-bit players. The real games start later." He drew a roll of bills from his pocket, peeled off two twenties, and handed one to Charles and one to Cassie. "Take these to a teller and get change for the slot machines. Maybe lady luck will be with you and you'll hit the jackpot."

Sonya glided up to them. "You're not giving the children money to gamble, are you Jacques? How's your luck been going? Did you win? The play was delightful. One of those frothy, old musicals that makes you feel light and happy. James and Lisa are waiting in the midnight-buffet line. Not that I'm hungry. But everything looks so beautiful. Cassie, you look exhausted. And you and Lisa are going snorkeling tomorrow. I'm so glad that nice young man, Larson, will be in charge. He seems very capable. Jacques? Charles? Are you coming with us to the buffet?"

"Thank you, Sonya," said Jacques, sliding his eyes to his Rolex, "but—"

"Here comes Professor Ornard," she cried, interrupting him. "Look at that outfit! Even in evening clothes, he's colorful."

Cassie, Charles, and Jacques turned to look at Philippe Ornard, who was walking toward them, a bright red-and-yellow plaid cummerbund and tie accenting his tuxedo. He raised a hand in greeting, then unexpectedly veered right behind a cluster of slot machines. As he turned away, Cassie noted his now-familiar gesture—right hand rubbing the ring on his left hand.

"That's strange," said Sonya. "I'm sure he was coming over to us. Perhaps someone called to him. Do you know him, Jacques? Philippe Ornard. He's an authority on gems."

"And ghosts and superstitions," said Charles. "He's the one who told us about Maiden's Hill."

Jacques straightened his lapels and his shoulders. A slight frown creased his forehead. "I don't know the man at all. And I don't believe I've ever heard of him, but . . . he did look familiar."

Sonya snickered. "He's hard to miss. He's always so outlandishly dressed."

After the buffet, Cassie and Charles, with Lisa trailing behind them, dragged along the corridor to their staterooms. Cassie had nibbled at a piece of chocolate cake and watched in amazement as Charles swallowed forkful after forkful of salads, cold cuts, and desserts.

"Charles, did your mother ever talk about Jacques?" Cassie asked.

Charles laughed. "She said he was kind of bossy even though he was younger."

"Did she like him?" Cassie persisted.

"I guess so. He was her only cousin. She did say his parents spoiled him. They were in their forties when he was born. I guess they were thrilled to have a child. His mother died about six years ago. I remember when my mother got the letter. Her uncle wrote to tell her. Grandfather never did."

After a moment, Cassie whispered, "Are you going to show Jacques the ring?"

"Sure . . . if he asks."

"What about the secret panel?"

"No," Charles said, thoughtfully. "Grandfather sent the ring to my mother and the letter to me. I don't know if Jacques knows about the secret or not, but I don't think I should tell him."

"Good," said Cassie. "The fewer people who know about the secret panel the better."

"Right," said Charles. Taking her hand and pulling her toward him, he slipped an arm around her shoulders. "You and I will solve the mystery when we get to Martinique."

"Hey, Charles," Lisa said, yawning, in back of them. "Are you coming snorkeling with us tomorrow?"

"No way. Larson's not my favorite person.

Anyway, Jacques and I plan to spend the day together."

Lisa, shoes in hand, a smear of chocolate on a pink ruffle, pushed past them, jabbing Cassie with her elbow. "Come on, Cassie. I want to get to bed," she complained.

"Okay, Lisa," said Cassie, acutely aware of the warmth of Charles's hand on her shoulder.

"We passed your room," said Cassie.

"I thought I'd see you ladies to your door," Charles said, tightening his arm around Cassie's shoulders. "Hey, your door's open a little."

The two of them stood looking at the slightly open door.

"What's the big deal?" Lisa groused. "Larson probably didn't close it tight after he made up the room." She shoved past them, pushed the door open, and switched on the light.

Her scream made Cassie's heart pound. She and Charles crowded into the room behind Lisa.

"My God!" Charles exclaimed.

"Oh no," groaned Cassie. Her nerves tightened in response to the violent assault on the room. Bureau drawers had been emptied onto the floor. Luggage was opened and tossed onto the bed. Clothes, powder, and makeup, had been thrown helter-skelter.

"The ring!" Charles cried.

Cassie shot to the closet, searched frantically in the pile of clothes on the floor for the shorts she'd been wearing that day, and delved into the pocket. Empty.

"Is it there?" Charles asked.

Cassie, eyes wide, pupils dilated, stared at him. "It's gone," she said in a low voice. Then, turning on her heel and rushing from the room, she cried, "The panel!" Charles's door was also ajar. The three of them crowded into the room and gaped at the mayhem.

"Charles, where did you hide the panel?" asked Cassie.

Charles opened his jacket. "Cassie, it's all right. I have it right here in my inner pocket. I'm keeping it with me. I even sleep with it."

"What's going on? Why would anyone do this to our rooms? What are you two talking about?" Lisa wailed.

"Someone stole Charles's ring," said Cassie.

"What's so special about that ring, anyway? Jacques said it wasn't worth much. . . . I'll get Daddy Jim and Mom. They'll know what to do."

Charles grabbed her by the arm as she backed from the room. "No, you can't."

Lisa, mouth open, stared at him.

"Charles is right," said Cassie. "Don't you see? If you tell them, they'll never let us go to the plantation."

Lisa knuckled tears from her eyes, smearing black streaks of mascara. "But Cassie, our room's been wrecked. We have to tell them."

"Do you want to go to the plantation?" Cassie's voice was iron.

Lisa sniffed and nodded.

"Then let's clean up the room and get to bed," Cassie ordered, sounding more resolute than she felt.

Much later that night, Cassie, nerves strung like a wire, lay in her narrow cot, listening to Lisa's rhythmic breathing. Eyes wide open in the dark, she wondered who had stolen the ring. Was it the professor? She remembered the incident in the casino. Why had he turned away? Or was it Enrico? Or Larson? Charles suspected Larson; he figured that he was working for the professor. Was it possible? What about Enrico? What had Fernando said? Enrico needed money. His wife was expecting another baby—their seventh.

Cassie shivered and rolled onto her side, trying to get comfortable. Thoughts and images churned in her brain.

The pulse and sway of the ship lulled the tenseness from her body. Tomorrow, snorkeling on Little Martinique. With Larson. Could it be Larson?

Cassie fell into a troubled sleep and dreamed of a shadowy figure stalking her.

Chapter 10

Shore Excursion

Little Martinique. Caribbean Cruise Lines' own private island.

Enjoy the day exploring every nook and cranny of this tropical paradise and join Caribbean Cruise Lines' staff of expert instructors for the exciting sport of snorkeling. Beginner and advanced all-day tours are available. A snorkel, mask, and fins are included in the tour price. Contact the cruise director's office for more information.

The anchored ship rested on glass-smooth, sky-blue water. Cassie leaned against the railing, and gazed at the strip of white beach fronting a softly rolling mountain range. She welcomed the hot sun pouring from the cloudless sky, its heat warming her, burning away the chill that remained from troubled dreams. She still couldn't believe the ring was gone. But the thief didn't have the secret panel. At least Charles still had that.

The ship's horn blasted the air. Cassie checked her watch. Almost time to meet Lisa.

Sonya's concise footsteps and brisk voice broke into her reverie. In white slacks and a blue-and-white top, she looked elegant and cool. "Cassie, there you are. Lisa's ready to go. The first group will be leaving in twenty minutes. You'd better hurry. They'll be a rush of people to leave the ship."

Cassie indicated the beach bag at her feet. "I'm all set."

Sonya's manicured hand touched Cassie's arm. "You two have a good time. But be careful. I'm glad that nice young man, Larson, is one of the instructors."

"We'll be careful, Sonya. Don't worry," said Cassie. She picked up her bag and left to join Lisa.

Larson. Charles's warning of last night seemed unreal in the hot, bright sun.

As Cassie and Lisa filed onto the tender, Lisa elbowed Cassie. "There's the gem guy, in another wild-colored outfit," she hissed.

Cassie saw the professor slouched against the tender's railing, arms spread out, hands clutching the top rail. A bright purple, yellow, and blue patterned shirt hung over his bulging belly and green shorts. He nodded at them, and his long upper lip stretched into a smile above his chins. His eyes were hidden behind sunglasses. Why had he avoided talking to them last night? Had he, seeing they weren't in their staterooms, rushed down to ransack their rooms? Did he have the ring? Was it on him now? Was it secreted someplace in his room?

Cassie looked the other way and hurried to the far side of the tender.

The professor heaved himself from the railing and wove through the other passengers to crowd next to them. "So, you two are going snorkeling, eh?"

Cassie, unconsciously drawing back from him, nodded. "Are you going?" she asked.

"No. No. I haven't been in years. I'm just going to enjoy the beach."

Larson's voice boomed from the front of the tender. "Morning, everybody. Those of you who are going snorkeling, stop at the Scuba Shack for your equipment. If anyone has any questions, check with me or Tom," he said, pointing to the other instructor.

Lisa giggled. "Larson is so hot! I hope we get in his group."

Cassie glanced over at Larson. She had to admit he was pretty cute—blond, blue-eyed, tall, and powerfully built. But Charles was sure he was working with the professor. Cassie gripped the rail to steady herself as the small boat rocked in the waves.

Larson spotted them and walked over, lurching against Cassie as the boat dipped. Did she imagine it or did his hands linger longer than necessary on her arms as he regained his balance? He grinned and said, "Sorry about that. So you decided to take me up on snorkeling. Did Charlie give you permission?"

Cassie bristled. "I don't need permission from him."

Larson's grin widened. "I thought maybe he'd staked a claim on you. First time snorkeling for you, right? And her too?" he asked, nodding at Lisa.

"Me too," said Lisa, flushing.

"You'll come with my group, Cassie. You did

say you're a strong swimmer, didn't you?" His voice challenged her.

Cassie raised her chin. "Yes. I'm a strong swimmer," she said, meeting his challenge.

Larson's eyes were a startling blue against his deep tan. "That's good. I told you before I'd teach you how to snorkel. Nothing to it, really." His gaze held Cassie's. She felt heat flooding her face. Why did he make her feel this way? Uneasy, yet flattered. He left, elbowing his way to the front of the tender.

Out of the corner of her eye she saw Professor Ornard turn to answer someone's greeting. Why, he and Larson hadn't even spoken to each other. In fact, they hadn't even looked at each other. It couldn't have been Larson the professor was talking to on the sports deck.

At the Scuba Shack, Larson handed Cassie her equipment. She and Lisa then hopped and sprinted over the burning sand to stand at the water's edge. Larry and Sally Johnson, a young couple they had talked to on the tender, showed them how to fit the mask.

"It's got to seal properly," said Sally. "Otherwise, water will leak in."

Lisa pulled the mask over her head, tangling it in her blond hair. "My hair's caught!" she squealed.

Larry laughed. "Help her out, Sally. Want some help with yours, Cassie? Let's see if I can tighten it for you. It looks a little big." Larry took the mask from her and adjusted the strap that went around her head. "That should take care of it," he said, handing it back. "Come on, let's go. Tom's giving instructions."

Tom swept the air with his arm and pointed to a cluster of rocks. "There's plenty to see just beyond that first group of rocks. Most of you won't go any farther. Advanced swimmers may want to go around that farther cluster. It's deeper, and you'll see more fish. Larson will lead that group."

Tom picked up his equipment from the sand. "Okay. Let's get wet. We'll practice using the snorkel and fins close to shore."

Larson splashed over to Cassie. "Come on, Cassie, my group is down there," he said, inclining his head toward four other people, three women and a man.

Cassie hesitated, looking at Lisa. She and Sally had their masks and snorkels on and were dipping their heads in and out of shoulder-high water.

"You said you were a strong swimmer," Larson said, his eyes daring her.

Cassie chewed at her bottom lip. Why was Larson so insistent she join his group? But then, why should she hesitate? She was a good swimmer. Maybe a little out of practice. She hadn't swum since last summer. Ignoring a prickling of unease, she followed Larson, splashing along the water's edge.

Larson called to the other four in the group, "You folks just warm up near the shore while I explain to the young lady how to use the snorkel." Taking the snorkel from Cassie's hands, he said, "It's a cinch, Cassie." Pointing to each part of the tube, he explained, "You clamp your teeth over this, the mouthpiece. It fits between the outside of your teeth and the inside of your lips. Your mouth forms a seal."

Larson's professional manner relaxed Cassie. She clamped her teeth around the mouthpiece and wriggled it about to make it more comfortable. Pulling it from her mouth, she said, "Mine looks different from yours. Mine's shaped like a J."

"You've got one of the older ones. It doesn't matter. Now get your fins on and try it in the water."

Cassie held the snorkel in her hands. "Does this have a purge valve—to let the water out?" she asked.

"Cassie, we don't have all day. Let's move it. The others are waiting," Larson snapped.

"But, Larson, what if water gets in this thing? Sally Johnson showed me the purge valve on hers."

Larson grabbed the snorkel from Cassie's hands and looked at it. "Okay. There isn't a purge valve. If any water gets in, you just blow it back out." He rolled his eyes and shook his head, making her feel like a pesky kid.

Cassie, the water washing about her, looked back at the other group. I could go with them, she thought. Do I really want to go out so deep?

"Cassie, put the fins on. What's the matter—getting cold feet?" Larson jeered, then, sloshing into the water, swam toward the others.

Cassie glared after him. "How about changing snorkels with me?" she shouted. He either didn't hear her or chose to ignore her as he swam out.

Cassie slipped the fins on. She had no trouble with them. She'd used them before. Doing a backward shuffle, she joined the group waiting for her.

Cassie soon forgot her anxieties and began to relax as she discovered beautiful plants and schools of fish below the surface of the clear, aquamarine sea. The magnifying effect of the water enhanced the magic of the wonderland. A bright-colored fish swam by, seeming to return her stare.

Occasionally Larson stopped and, removing his snorkel and treading water, pointed out an exotic fish or a coral reef. Gradually, as the sun rose higher in the sky, they left the safety of the shore behind them.

Cassie fell behind the others. She began to feel chilled and tired. She swam on, following the fins some distance ahead of her. She raised her head to sight the rocks. Still a ways out. To her surprise, the swimmer ahead of her suddenly stood in the water. It was Marie, an older woman.

Cassie swam to the sandbar, pulled the snorkel from her mouth, and cleared her mask of water. She shivered, welcoming the hot sun on her head and shoulders.

Marie's smile was warm and friendly. "It's lovely, isn't it?"

"Oh, yes," Cassie breathed. "It's beautiful out here. And this sandbar is great for resting. I wonder if there are more along the way?"

Marie bobbed about in the shoulder-deep water. "No, I've been here before, and this is the only one. Once we leave it, it's a long way to the rocks." Shielding her eyes against the glare of sun on water, she searched the ocean for the other swimmers. "There they are," she said, pointing to the rocks. "I guess we're a couple of slowpokes." She slid her gear into place.

Cassie bit back the impulse to ask Marie to swim back to shore with her. After all, she wasn't a quitter. She watched Marie submerge. Soon she could see only her snorkel and an occasional glimpse of shoulder. She looked back at the shore—so far away. She put her mask on, clamped her teeth around the harsh mouthpiece, and followed.

Past the rocks, still in the confines of the bay but closer to the open sea, Cassie swam through short, choppy waves. Air flowed imperfectly through the J-shaped snorkel. She longed to take a full, deep breath. The deeper, colder water and fatigue numbed her limbs.

To her right the sea stretched endlessly. To her left rose the rocks, black and menacing, blocking any view of the shore. A hard knot of fear grew in her stomach. Where was Marie? She and everyone else had disappeared.

Panic tightening every muscle, Cassie struck forward, thrusting one arm after the other through the heavy sea. Water flooded her ears, nose, and mouth. She'd gone too far under, submerging the snorkel. I won't panic. I won't panic, she thought.

She lifted her head and puffed frantically through the tube to clear it.

Water squirted back into Cassie's mouth. The harder she puffed, the less air she had. Air! Air! She needed air. The snorkel suffocated her. She ripped it off. She ripped off the mask. Free. She gulped mouthfuls of air. A wave washed over her. She choked. Coughing and gagging, she thrashed wildly with her arms.

A huge shape loomed in front of her, its eyes bulging behind the water-magnified lens of the mask. Larson. Cassie grabbed for him, but he avoided her, swam behind her, and approached her from the back.

Cassie felt his arm go around her head, his hip under her shoulder. Spots swam before her eyes. Tired. So tired. Larson's voice, sounding muffled, floated to her. "Cassie, you're all right. Relax. Just relax."

Riding higher in the water, able to breathe, Cassie calmed down. Larson changed position. Floating on his back, he placed a hand on either side of her head, then kicked toward the rocks.

Larson dragged her onto a large, sloping rock that stood apart from the others. Cassie lay there, shivering in the warmth of the sun, getting her strength and her breath back.

A shadow fell over her. Larson leaned toward her. Light shot off his short spiked hair. His face drew closer; she felt his warm breath, smelled the sea salt. Contradictory emotions swirled through Cassie. Larson had just saved her life. She should be grateful. Instead, a rush of panic rose in her throat. She pushed against his chest, struggling to escape him. He pressed her down, his mouth covering hers in a rough kiss.

Cassie heaved herself sideways and jumped up, wiping her mouth with her hand. "What are you doing? Where is everybody?" she gasped.

Larson draped his forearms over his bent knees and stared at her. "They're resting on one of the big rocks. I signaled them that I had you. They'll assume you're resting till we join them. We're all alone, Cassie, where no one can see us."

Cassie's hazel eyes flashed, and she tossed her head back. "They won't expect us to be here long."

"What I have to say won't take long," said Larson.

Cassie scrambled up the rock, scraping her knee.

Larson watched her; then, his voice mimicking hers, said, "I thought you were a 'strong swimmer.'"

Cassie flushed. He had set her up, goaded her into joining his group.

Larson hunched his shoulders and swung his arms. His voice mocking, he said, "Too bad you got that old snorkel. I thought we'd gotten rid of those things—those J-shaped, small-bore snorkels. They don't have good air space. Makes it harder to breathe. But I guess you know that now—don't you?"

Fury rushed through Cassie. She put her hands on her hips. "You made sure I got that useless snorkel, didn't you? I could have drowned."

"But you didn't. I made sure of that, too."

"Thanks a lot," said Cassie. "What do you want, anyway?"

Larson, looking away from her, said, "I want money, Cassie. I need it to settle some messy business I left back home. And you and your friend Charlie have a piece of jewelry a lot of people are interested in. I get it from you and sell it to the highest bidder."

"It was you who followed us to the museum, wasn't it?" said Cassie. "Charles said it was you. You could have killed me . . . throwing me against that building." She shivered, despite the hot sun pouring down on her.

Larson laughed. "Don't be so dramatic. If I wanted to hurt you, I could do it easily. And I will . . . if I have to."

Cassie looked into Larson's cold blue eyes. She believed him. He would hurt her to get what he wanted. She took a deep breath, and said, "But you've got the ring. You stole it last night. So what do you want now?"

"There's something missing from that ring. Before I turn it over to the highest bidder, I want the small panel that fits in there."

Cassie's mind raced. Maybe Larson would tell her who wanted the ring. She knew the professor wanted it, but who else? "You said 'highest bidder,' Larson. How many people want the ring, and who are they?"

Larson's fingers bit into her shoulders. "Listen, Cassie, I ask the questions, not you. I want that panel. The ring alone can't be worth much. The panel must be a clue. So far, I've taken all the risks, but whomever I sell it to is going to have to include me in the jackpot."

"A great plan," Cassie said sarcastically.

Larson shook her. "Shut up," he snarled. "You get that panel to me today, or else—"

"You're out of luck," said Cassie, struggling to escape his grasp. "We lost it in Puerto Rico."

Larson stared into her eyes. "You'd better be telling me the truth," he threatened. He released her and squinted toward the horizon. Turning back, he said, "You're the one who's out of luck. I can still sell the ring. Whoever gets it won't know about the missing panel until I'm long gone. Then they'll be looking for you and boyfriend, Charlie."

Larson slid into the water and swam toward the rock where the rest of the group waited. Cassie stood alone, listening to the slap of water on stone, then, with a shiver, slipped into the cold water to follow him.

Chapter 11

Shore Excursion

Martinique—a bit of France in the blue Caribbean.

Called the "Island of Flowers," this romantic land produces lilies, orchids, and bougainvilleas among coconut groves, tree ferns, and stalks of bamboo.

The island is mountainous, especially in the rain-forested northern part, where Mount Pelée rises 4,656 feet.

The irregular coastline provides five bays, dozens of coves, and miles of sandy beaches.

Capital: Fort-de-France, 45,000 inhabitants.

Official language: French—but most people speak the local Creole patois.

CLIMATE: The average temperature is 75 to 85 degrees Fahrenheit. At higher elevations, it is considerably cooler.

ARRIVE: Thursday, 8:00 A.M.

DEPART: Saturday, 2:00 P.M.

For group tours, apply in the cruise director's office.

The Jeep sped along Martinique's well-paved roads, leaving behind the crowded boutique-lined streets of Fort-de-France and the stretches of white beaches bordered with palm trees. The road leapfrogged from hill to hill. Occasionally, Cassie could see the sea far below, deeply blue and dotted with islets.

That's how Little Martinique looks from a distance, she thought. She swallowed against the anger and fear that rose in her throat. Yesterday, back on shore, Larson acting the hero. And the professor. She shuddered, and felt again his arm draped around her shoulders, his heavy fingernails scraping her bare flesh, heard his sibilant whisper, "I'm glad you're all right." She had shrunk away from him, biting back angry words of accusation.

This morning, Claude Nobre had met them at the ship. With old-world grace, he had bowed low over the ladies' hands. Sonya had been delighted with the elderly man's charm and beamed approval of their visit. But Cassie's father had just smiled politely, asked for the Nobre Plantation phone number, and instructed the girls on how to contact the ship.

Finally, they were in Claude Nobre's Jeep, speeding toward Martinique's mountain region. Cassie glanced at Charles's profile as he sat beside his great-uncle in the front seat. He'd been terribly upset when she'd told him about Larson, accusing himself of putting her in danger. She had assured him they'd be safe once they were away from the professor and Larson. But now, though they were leaving them far behind, she couldn't shake a niggling sense of anxiety.

Thoughts kept whirling in her mind. Had Larson sold the ring yet? Who had he sold it to? Perhaps at this very moment, someone had the ring, someone suspected that she and Charles had unearthed its secret. What if . . . ?

Lisa's voice broke into her thoughts. "Oh, those flowers are so pretty! I wonder what kind they are."

Claude Nobre answered in accented but perfect English. "Those are bougainvillea. They are beautiful, are they not? We have a great many beautiful flowers here. Orchids, bougainvillea.

Much grows on the island. Orange, grapefruit, breadfruit trees."

Charles rubbed his bare arms. "It's colder up here, and windy."

His great-uncle nodded. "That is due to the trade winds. They are our air-conditioning. Look there, in the distance. You can see Mount Pelée."

Cassie saw the looming bulk of Mount Pelée but could not see its peak, for clouds formed and re-formed gloomily around the top.

"You have heard the story of Mount Pelée?" asked Claude Nobre in a somber voice. "In nineteen hundred and two it erupted and destroyed Saint-Pierre and all the people in it. Gases and steam burst from it and blacked out the sun. Within three minutes the eruption turned the city and harbor of Saint-Pierre into a flaming caldron. Thirty thousand people died . . ." His voice fell to a whisper. "And now Jerome, too, is dead—gone forever."

Charles shifted uncomfortably in his seat. "Grandfather wrote that he had heart trouble. Did he have a heart attack?" he asked.

Claude Nobre's head jerked toward Charles. Frowning, his voice harsh, he asked, "Did not Jacques tell you?"

Charles's eyebrows shot up. "Tell me what?"

Claude Nobre, his hands gripping the steering wheel, stared straight ahead. "Perhaps he did not want to upset you. But you should know the truth," he said, his voice uneven. "When your grandfather's body was found, there was evidence of a struggle—bruises, furniture overturned. Jerome's heart pills were spilled all over the desk. It looked as though he had been trying to reach them." He paused, then released a shuddering breath. "The police are awaiting the results of the autopsy. Perhaps we will know more then."

Cassie shifted uneasily. She heard Lisa's sharp intake of breath, and knew from the rigid set of Charles's shoulders, the little muscles bulging along his jawline, that he was too upset to speak. An image of the Jeweled Jesu flashed before her. How was the statue connected to the Nobre family? She thought of Charles's grandfather lying dead and of all the people killed in the volcanic eruption.

No one spoke. Cassie heard the wind moaning through the trees. She leaned forward in her seat. "Mr. Nobre, was anything left after the volcano erupted?" she asked. "Anything at all?"

Claude Nobre nodded curtly. "Yes. A few things were found. There is a museum in Saint-Pierre that has some relics. They are rather grim. There are some nails that were melted and fused together, a bunch of keys welded into one mass, cinders—once books or food—and a poor box from a church with the coins run together."

Was that the same church, Cassie wondered, that the Jeweled Jesu was from? But no, that was another church on the outskirts of town.

Cassie shivered, but not from the wind. Here on the island the story of the Jeweled Jesu seemed more real. And the suspicion that Charles's grandfather might have been killed . . . was there a connection?

Claude Nobre turned off the well-paved road onto a narrow, twisting one. Lush green vegetation, reeking of decay, surrounded them, sometimes giving way to a glimpse of a valley far below. Through tall, dark-leaved trees, Cassie caught sight of a white shadowy form. The next minute, they were driving through a fine mist.

Cassie laughed nervously. "I thought I saw a ghost," she said. "But it was only mist."

Lisa, who had moved closer to Cassie and grabbed her arm, giggled and moved away. "I did, too, Cassie," she said.

Claude Nobre did not laugh. "We are actually going through a small cloud. We are pretty high up, and clouds cap the mountains nearly every afternoon. But we do have our local ghost."

It was graveyard quiet. No one said a word. Cassie's mind leaped to the story of Maiden's Hill. Was it really haunted? Or was Mr. Nobre teasing them?

Charles, his voice muffled in the eerie stillness, asked, "You mean the ghost of Maiden's Hill?"

Claude Nobre nodded. "I see Jacques has filled you in on our local lore."

"Do you believe a ghost is really there?" asked Charles.

His great-uncle shrugged. "I myself have never encountered a ghost. But then, I have not been there at night. Some people say they have felt an icy chill or have sensed a thickening of the atmosphere. Others say they have seen strange lights. Research into phantom encounters indicates these are indeed signs of phantoms—or ghosts."

He expertly guided the Jeep around a twisting curve. Reaching branches poked through the open window, brushing Charles's then Cassie's arms. Claude Nobre's solemn voice continued. "Supposedly, a violent death can cause a spirit to linger at the scene of its murder. If you know the story of Maiden's Hill, you know of the Carib's massacre of the Arawaks and the slaying of the young maiden's betrothed. According to legend, they never did find the girl's body."

Charles, ducking to avoid another grasping branch, said, "Jacques said Maiden's Hill is near the plantation."

"Yes. It is not far, but it is quite a steep climb. It is in one of the *mornes*. That is what we call the high hills that rise among the mountains."

Cassie leaned forward, grasping the back of the seat to keep her balance. "I'd love to see it. It sounds so mysterious."

Charles quickly added, "Me too. Cassie doesn't have much time here. Maybe we can go there tomorrow."

Claude Nobre wheeled the Jeep around another curve. "I suppose you could. Maybe I can spare a worker to take you."

"That's not necessary, Uncle Claude. I'm sure we can find it."

Claude Nobre nodded. "I am sure I have an old hiking map of the area. It is a fantastic view from up there. You can take a lunch and picnic in the meadow."

"What about the ghost?" asked Lisa.

A flicker of a smile crossed Claude Nobre's face. "As I said, no one has ever seen the ghost during the day," he assured her.

Cassie slumped back. Lisa. How could they search for the Jeweled Jesu with her there?

"What's the cave like?" asked Charles.

"It is a tube cave. It was formed hundreds or even thousands of years ago from hot molten lava. The outside hardens, forming a crust, or roof. The hot, inner part drains out, leaving a tube behind."

"Is it deep?" asked Cassie.

"It is long, but it is not deep. Tube caves are never far from the surface. Perhaps, Charles, sometime during your visit, you and I can explore the cave."

They left the mist behind and passed through fields. Claude Nobre cleared his throat. "We have entered Nobre land, Charles," he said. "These are sugarcane fields." He pointed to an ancient building. "That is our distillery. It was built in eighteen hundred and twenty-five. It is there that the juice is squeezed from the sugarcane to make rum."

He turned onto an unpaved road, almost a track, and then onto a long, rutted drive. After a time, the foliage cleared, and before them stood a gloomy, two-story house, shaded by the deep green glossy leaves of mango trees.

Claude Nobre climbed from the Jeep. He was tall and slim like Jacques, but with a sinewy, muscular build that spoke of hard physical labor. His dark eyes were deeply set, and vertical lines ran from either side of his nose past his mouth. He turned those dark, watchful eyes on Charles and, gesturing to the house with a work-worn hand, asked, "What do you think of the Nobre Plantation, Charles? Is it what you expected?"

Charles studied the imposing structure. The house, made from mahogany boards that had aged, was silver-gray. Panes of beveled glass made the entry door look handsome, but an unkempt aura hung over the house and grounds.

Claude Nobre nodded tersely. "It is a little run down, is it not? It could be beautiful again. But it would take much money, and money . . ." He shrugged expressively and led them up crumbling stone steps.

They stood awkwardly in the faded but well-proportioned center hall, where Mr. Nobre had told them to wait. Charles, hands hanging loosely by his sides, a frown creasing his forehead, studied a series of oils that depicted the harvesting of sugarcane.

Cassie went to stand beside him. "Charles," she said in a low voice, "do you think whoever gets the ring will follow us out here?"

"No," said Charles thoughtfully. "I don't think so. Even if the professor suspects there was a clue in the ring, he can't know for sure. And he doesn't know we have it."

"But Larson said there were two or more bidders for the ring. Who else could know about it?"

Charles shrugged. "I don't think there's anyone else. Larson probably made that up."

Cassie chewed her lower lip. "Why would he do that?"

Lisa, peering into a room off the hall, interrupted their whispered conversation, saying, "This place gives me the creeps."

Mr. Nobre and a thin, dark-skinned woman walked up the long hall from a back room. He introduced her as Madame Maria Bonne and told them to get their luggage from the Jeep while he instructed her as to which rooms they would have.

Before showing them to their rooms, Madame Bonne, talking in a combination of the island patois and broken English, gave them a tour of the house. A jalousied porch encircled both floors, cooling and darkening the rooms. Downstairs, to the right of the center hall, running front to back, were the living room, dining room, and kitchen. Opposite them were three other rooms: the front sitting room, the library, and Claude Nobre's office.

Jerome Nobre's office had been in what was once a guest cottage a short distance from the house. "Police close it," Madame Bonne said, bowing her head and making the sign of the cross.

Cassie shuddered. The cottage must be where Charles's grandfather's body had been found. Murdered? Who could have murdered him? A sudden thought struck terror in her heart. Could the murderer be the other bidder for the ring?

Cassie, her heart racing, followed the others upstairs, where four rooms ran front to back on either side of the stairway. Madame Bonne ushered Lisa into the second bedroom on the left, and Cassie into the third room. She then led Charles to the right back bedroom.

In her room, Cassie unpacked the few things she had brought with her and placed them in a dresser drawer. Then, hands on slim hips, she looked about the room. Grayish, once white, stucco walls. A dark but faded green spread matched the drapes covering the French doors. She opened the doors and stepped out onto the porch. Late afternoon light filtered through the jalousies. Toward the back, a section of wooden slats was missing. Here, branches of a mango tree groped for the house. Cassie listened to the breeze sigh through its leaves, heard the scratching of its branches. A heavy sense of foreboding settled in her chest.

Dinner, chicken and yams, served in the musty dining room, was a dismal affair, far different from the sumptuous, elegantly served meals on board ship. At first, Claude Nobre made an effort to talk to his young great-nephew and guests, but, with frequent glances at the empty place set for Jacques, he soon sank into silence. The strident ring of the phone shattered the stillness.

Madame Bonne hurried in. "Monsieur Jacques, Monsieur Nobre."

Mr. Nobre wiped his mouth with his napkin, placed the napkin by his plate, and excused himself, saying, "Perhaps we will find out why my son could not join us for dinner tonight."

Lisa, extracting a half-chewed piece of chicken from her mouth and hiding it under her roll, said, "What are we going to do while we're here, Charles? Maybe we should go back to the boat. There're no beaches or anything up here."

"But, Lisa . . . ," Cassie said.

Claude Nobre's voice had been growing steadily louder. Now he shouted, "No!

Absolutely not!" and slammed the phone down.

A moment later he appeared in the doorway, red-faced, sliding a finger in the neck of his too-tight shirt collar. "Children, you will have to excuse me. I have some business to attend to. Charles, when you have finished, please come to my office. I would like to talk with you. Not now," he said as Charles started to rise from his seat. "Finish dinner with the young ladies. Madame Bonne has prepared a sweet. Good night, Cassandra, Lisa."

"Some sweet," grumbled Lisa, following Cassie up the stairs. "It tasted more like glue than bread pudding."

"'Night, Lisa," said Cassie, anxious to be alone with her thoughts, wondering if Charles would tell his great-uncle about the ring's secret panel.

Lisa followed Cassie into her room. "I don't like this place," she whined. "It's dark and spooky, and the food's awful." She plopped down on Cassie's bed.

"It will look better tomorrow in the daylight," said Cassie, toying with a hairbrush. "I'm really tired. I think I'll go to bed now."

Lisa lay still as a stone on the bed, watching the shadow of the ceiling fan that turned around and around. She snorted. "What were you and Charles whispering about in the hall, Cassie? I bet he's coming up here later."

Cassie's nerves were stretched tight. The helplessness and fear she'd felt when Larson threatened her; her father's remoteness; and an ever-present anxiety heightened her tension and made her irritable.

She stood at the foot of the bed, clenching her fists and staring at Lisa. "You're such a pest, Lisa," she said.

Lisa stretched, then folded her hands beneath her head. "I'm going to call Daddy Jim tomorrow," she threatened. "I don't want to stay here."

Cassie gripped the bedpost, then flopped over to a chair. She knew her father wouldn't let her stay alone. "All right, Lisa," she said through clenched teeth. "What do you want?"

Lisa sat up quickly and brushed the hair from her eyes. "I want you to tell me what you and Charles are always whispering about. What's going on, anyway? You always leave me out. It isn't fair."

Cassie stared at Lisa, recognizing the anger in her voice and surprised by something else—the hurt. Hurt because she felt left out. Cassie knew what being left out felt like. Hadn't her own father left her out? But Lisa was a pest. Cassie tossed her head and said, "You're just a troublemaker, Lisa."

Lisa's voice rose. "You're the troublemaker, Cassie. Right from the beginning, you didn't want to share a room with me."

"Why should I? You make such a mess. I can never find anything."

Lisa lowered her voice. "You're just jealous because your father's my father now. He lives with me and my mother. Not you."

Cassie felt as though she'd been hit in the stomach. Her throat constricted, and tears threatened to overflow. She blinked furiously, took a deep breath, and swallowed. "As far as I'm concerned, he's not my father anymore. You can have him. I didn't want to come on this dumb trip in the first place."

Lisa, her face mottled and red, stood up, hands on hips. "Do you think . . . ?" A light knock on the door interrupted her. She smirked at Cassie. "I suppose that's Charles now."

Cassie, heart thumping in her chest, opened the door, and Charles, face flushed and dark eyes wide, stepped in. He took Cassie by the shoulders. "Cassie, wait till you hear—" He stopped short when he saw Lisa.

Lisa stomped toward the door. "I'm going to call Daddy Jim and my mother right now. I don't want to stay here."

"You can't do that," cried Charles. "Cassie will have to leave, too."

"Lisa, wait," Cassie called, "let's talk this over." She turned to Charles. "Lisa wants to know about the secret."

Lisa, hands on hips, bottom lip thrust out, stood waiting.

Charles, eyes narrowed, stared at her intently. "Can you keep a secret, Lisa?"

Her eyes opened wide. "Sure, I can."

Charles nodded and ran his hands through his dark curls. "Okay. Sit down and I'll tell both of you what my great-uncle said tonight. Cassie can fill you in on the rest later. Actually, it's best you know, because you'll have to come with us tomorrow."

Lisa plopped on the edge of the bed and leaned forward, her weight on her hands. Cassie sat in the chair, hands on knees, waiting expectantly.

"My great-uncle took me into his office at the back of the house. You know the room. Madame Bonne pointed it out this afternoon. It's awfully dark in there—dark furniture, dark wall hangings. He had only one small desk lamp lit. He told me to sit in this huge maroon leather chair. Then he paced back and forth with his hands clasped behind his back. Sometimes he hardly seemed to know I was there."

Charles took a deep breath and began. Cassie listened intently, picturing the scene, feeling as though she were there.

Claude Nobre stood a moment with his back to Charles, then turned and fixed his dark gaze on him. "Charles, I am going to tell you something that happened many years ago—long before you were born. Before your grandfather and I were born. But that event reaches out to affect us even now. It is true," he murmured, "that the sins of the father are visited on the children."

He wiped his hands across his eyes, then continued. "On May eighth, nineteen hundred and two, disaster struck Martinique. As I told you earlier today, Mount Pelée exploded in a burst of ash and steam and destroyed the town of Saint-Pierre. In three minutes, thirty thousand people were dead. And, as if that were not bad enough, another eruption occurred on May twentieth, completing the destruction."

Charles sat in the deep chair and listened to his great-uncle.

"Everything was destroyed. Everything. A bustling city stopped, just like that." Claude Nobre snapped his fingers and shook his head. "But, outside the town, there was a church that stood on a rise of ground. Miraculously, it was left standing. Nothing inside was damaged. But, strangely, something was missing." A long sigh shuddered through him. "Something of great beauty and great value—a silver statue of Christ surrounded by twelve precious stones."

"The Jeweled Jesu," Charles breathed.

Claude's piercing eyes studied Charles. "You know about it?" he asked sharply.

Charles shifted uneasily in the chair. "A man on the ship gave a lecture on gemstones. There's a picture of the Jeweled Jesu on the cover of his book," he explained.

Claude Nobre nodded, then continued pacing. "The Jeweled Jesu had disappeared. As I said, it had great value and the church searched for it—but in vain. Stories circulated about it. Stories circulated of ill fortune befalling the thief and his family for generation after generation. Your grandfather and I grew up hearing these stories, but they were nothing more than that—just stories." His face and body sagged. His voice a mere whisper, he said, "Until that fateful day so many years ago when we found it."

Charles leaned forward. "You and Grandfather found the Jeweled Jesu?"

Claude Nobre nodded and stared straight ahead. "Long ago, before your mother was born. The distillery—the building we passed today—needed repairs. Beneath it is a storage room full of odds and ends. For some reason, on that particular day, Jerome felt adventurous. He climbed down there and poked through all the debris. After a time, he shouted to me to join him. I remember the moment as though it were yesterday. I climbed into the musty hole and there stood Jerome, gazing in awe at the most beautiful statue we had ever seen. Jerome lifted it from its wrappings in an ancient trunk, and, even in that dim light, it glowed.

"We knew at once what it was. I was thrilled. Here was our chance to make a fortune. And we needed the money. Things had not been going well. The plantation was run down. . . . Now we could rebuild it." Claude's eyes blazed. For a moment, he resembled Jacques at the gaming tables, flushed and intent. Claude dropped his eyes and shook his head, sighing deeply.

"That was the beginning of a disagreement between your grandfather and me that was never resolved. And now that he is dead, it never will be.

"Right from the beginning, Jerome wanted to return the Jeweled Jesu to the church. He said it would be sacrilegious to dismantle it and sell the silver and jewels. That if we did so, we would be cursed. You see, he believed the stories we had heard as children. But at the time, I thought them to be only superstition. I couldn't see it. I only knew that we needed money and we had the means to a fortune in our hands. Since I was the older brother, Jerome would not return the statue to the church without my agreeing to it. But neither would he let me sell it. So, he hid it away, hoping that one day I would agree with him and, together, we would return the Jeweled Jesu to the church." Claude paced back and forth several times, saying nothing.

Breaking the silence, Charles asked, "Uncle Claude, did you ever find out how it got in the distillery?"

Another great sigh, seeming to come from his feet, shuddered through Claude. Sadness tinged his voice as he said, "We can only guess that our father took it—he would have been about seventeen at the time of the eruption. Or perhaps his father. But that is a mystery we will never solve. I only know that your grandfather found it in the cellar of the distillery, and that from that day, it drove a wedge between us."

Charles clutched the arms of the leather chair; his moist hands stuck to the smooth surface. "Why are you telling me this?" he asked.

Claude sat heavily in the desk chair and covered his face with his hands. Drawing a deep breath, he said, "Charles, as you know, there is a question as to how your grandfather died. There were signs of an argument in his office—furniture overturned, papers scattered."

Charles's face turned ashen. "You think it's true? You think he was murdered?"

Claude stared straight ahead. "The police are waiting for the autopsy results. Jerome had a heart condition for years, but . . ." He gestured helplessly.

Charles jumped up and clenched his fists. "Who could have done such a thing? Did anyone else know about the Jeweled Jesu?"

Claude opened his mouth, then, not meeting Charles's eyes, said, "I do not think anyone else knows . . . not for sure . . . but perhaps there is suspicion." His eyes flicked to Charles and away.

"Foolishly, a few months ago I made discreet inquiries as to the worth of the Jeweled Jesu. I never mentioned it by name, but . . . when I told Jerome how much money we could get, we had a terrible argument—a loud, ugly argument. We were in his office. At one point, I thought I heard someone outside. I checked, but saw no one. I do not think anyone heard us.

"Jerome was furious with me. That is when he told me you were bringing the secret to the Jeweled Jesu's hiding place with you, that you carried it in a ring he had sent to your mother. He said he had had the ring made in case he died unexpectedly, that he had wanted to mark the Jeweled Jesu's existence so that it would not be lost forever. He said you were the only one he could trust to retrieve the Jeweled Jesu; that he was too old to make the journey to do so; that, despite the fact that I was the older brother, he was going to go against my wishes and return the statue to the church."

They looked at each other in silence for a moment. The Claude continued. "That is why I called you in here, Charles. You have the answer ."

Charles hesitated, then asked, "What would you do with the Jeweled Jesu if you found it?"

"I'd return it to the church."

"You've changed your mind? You agree with my grandfather now, when you didn't last week?" Charles's voice rose with anger and suspicion.

Claude gripped Charles by the arms and looked directly into his eyes. "Yes, Charles. I changed my mind. Too late. Too late to tell my brother. But it was not until he was gone that I realized how wrong I had been, that there are things more important than money."

Charles swallowed hard. "That's what grandfather wrote in his letter—that he'd waited too long to patch things up with my mother, that he'd waited until it was too late. . . ."

"Yes. We both made mistakes," said Claude, releasing Charles. "But the ring, Charles. The garnet. I remember when Jerome had it made. I did not know then that it held the secret to the Jeweled Jesu. Bring me the ring, and together, you and I, we can discover its secret and return the statue to its rightful place. Then, your grandfather can rest in peace, and perhaps the Nobre Plantation, free of its curse, will flourish again."

Charles, rubbing his arms, backed away from his uncle. "I don't have the ring anymore."

Claude, his voice hoarse, echoed, "You do not have the ring?"

"No, I don't. I gave it to my friend, Cassie, to keep, because someone kept searching my room. Then, someone stole it from her room."

"Someone? Someone? Who is this someone?" Claude rasped.

Charles backed toward the door. "I don't know, Uncle Claude. Who else knows the ring is connected with the Jeweled Jesu?"

The question hung between them. Charles left the room, leaving his uncle looking like a very old man.

Cassie awoke with a start. Sleep had been fitful, bits and pieces of Charles's story invading her dreams. She lay still, suddenly alert, wondering what had woken her.

The French doors rattled, then swung slowly inward. Cassie froze, holding her breath. The doors swung to with a bang. She released her breath. It's just the wind, she thought. She slid from the bed and padded to the doors. Instead of fastening them, she stepped out onto the veranda.

A breeze rustled the leaves of the mango trees, which scratched its branches across the jalousies. Pungent odors filled the air. A tree frog croaked. Cassie walked to the back of the house, where the trees stood further back. She passed the room Madam Bonne had said was Jacques's. The side doors were closed, but the doors facing the back stood open.

Cassie wondered if Jacques was back. Not wanting to see him, she stood in the darkness of the corner. Chin in hands, elbows propped on the railing, she gazed down at the moonlit scene.

A great moon, nearly full, threw moving shadows from towering trees across the terrace. Underbrush, like small animals, crept across the crumbling stone.

How beautiful this place must have been! she thought. Maybe, if Charles and I find the Jeweled Jesu and return it to the church, the curse against the Nobre family will be lifted and the plantation will be beautiful again. . . . The curse? What am I thinking? Do I believe in curses?

A movement of light caught her eye. She peered into the dark tangle of trees that bordered the back of the terrace. There it was again. "The office," she murmured. "That's where Madame Bonne said the office was. That's where Charles's grandfather was found dead."

Impulsively, she slipped down the back stairs and across the terrace. Who was there in the dead of night? She had to know.

The moon sent its light through overhanging branches, partially illuminating the well-worn path. At times, thick shadows enveloped the path, slowing her progress. The stench of decaying vegetation rose from the woods, gagging her. Near the end of the track, something sharp scratched the sole of her bare foot. She gasped and, steadying herself against a tree, brushed her foot clean.

Behind her came the sound of voices. Confused, she slipped from the path and hid behind a giant mahogany tree. The voices came closer—two men, their flashlights held low, close to the ground. Cassie strained to hear them, but couldn't understand a word they said. They passed within a few feet of her.

Jacques, carrying a flashlight, emerged from the cottage just as the two men approached it. His surprised, angry voice told Cassie he hadn't expected them. The heavier of the two men grabbed Jacques and pinioned his arms back while the smaller one punched him repeatedly in the stomach, all the time uttering menacing sounds in a foreign language.

A vicious puff of wind sent icy fingers down Cassie's nightshirt, but perspiration prickled her armpits. Her mouth was dry, and she was frozen to the spot.

Jacques fell to the ground. The small man kicked at his ribs until the larger one pulled him away. They disappeared up the path.

Paralyzed, Cassie wondered what she should do. What would Jacques do to her if he knew she was there? Why had he been in the cottage—wasn't it closed off by the police? What if he was dead?

Jacques groaned and rolled to his knees. Cassie gagged when she heard him heave the contents of his stomach. She watched him get slowly to his feet and backtrack to the cottage door. He locked the door, then bent to retrieve his flashlight. Knowing he was all right, she fled back up the path to the safety of her room.

Chapter 12

After a breakfast of cold cereal and fruit, Madame Bonne handed them a package. "Mr. Nobre. He say I pack lunch. He leave map on hall table."

Charles packed the lunch in his knapsack. "Thank you, Madame Bonne. Where is my uncle?"

Madame Bonne smiled. "Already working. Already gone before you come down. Always up early, your uncle."

Cassie glanced up the stairs. "Jacques?" she asked. "Is he with Mr. Nobre?"

Madame Bonne sniffed. "That one. Never up early."

Outside, they studied the map. Cassie, peering

over Charles's shoulder, said, "I say we take the mountain path. It would take us forever to get there by the road. Look how it twists and doubles back and forth."

"The path looks awful steep," said Lisa.

Charles folded the map and stuffed it in his shirt pocket. "But it's much more direct. It looks like the path starts about a mile or so up the road. There should be a sign. Let's go."

They followed the winding road through thick foliage. Even though little sunlight filtered through the branches of giant trees, Cassie felt the mid-morning heat.

Lisa trudged along a few steps behind her. They had spoken to each other with cautious reserve this morning. Lisa's accusations and the realization that she, too, had been feeling left out made Cassie wonder: Had she been fair? Had she given friendship with Lisa a chance? After all, Lisa was younger.

Now Lisa moaned, "I'm hot. How long have we been walking?"

"We just started, Lisa," said Charles, adjusting the weight of his knapsack. "Hey, that looks like a sign up ahead."

Cassie heard the truck before she saw it. "Car coming," she called. The three of them scurried to the side of the road. The driver, a thin man with a mustache, waved to them.

Cassie stared after the truck as it rattled around a curve. "Who do you suppose that was?"

Charles shrugged. "Probably a neighbor. Why?"

Cassie glanced warily over her shoulder. "I'll be glad when we're off the main road."

"Some main road," muttered Lisa.

Charles's eyebrows knit together in a frown. "Why so jittery, Cassie?"

Cassie shrugged. She couldn't shake the vision of the two men beating Jacques. She wanted to tell Charles, but if Lisa heard, she might turn around, run back to the house, and call her mother and her "Daddy Jim."

"Here we go," said Charles, pointing to a weathered board nailed to a tree that read, in faint letters, MAIDEN'S HILL.

Lisa swept her heavy hair up, then let it fall back. "I don't think I want to go," she complained. "That doesn't look like much of a trail." She sat on a flat rock near a tree. "Just give me my lunch. I'll wait here."

Cassie slipped off one of the elastics from her ponytail. "Here, Lisa, put your hair up. It's cooler. You don't want to turn back now. Just think. We might find the Jeweled Jesu."

Lisa sighed, heaved herself to her feet, and followed Charles. Cassie came last. The path bore its way upward along the thickly wooded hillside, where underbrush whipped against her cotton slacks. Occasionally, the path opened onto fields of long grass and bracken. Here, a welcome breeze dried the sweat glistening on Cassie's face and dampening her shirt. At times, they passed over the twisting road. The going was slow. The backs of Cassie's thighs and calves began to pull.

Once again they crossed the road that was little more than a track and, with the help of a faded and splintered sign, found the nearly overgrown path on the other side. Cassie leaned into the steep grade and grabbed at trailing vines to pull herself upward. A mosquito buzzed her ear. She slapped at it and wiped the sweat from her brow.

Charles stopped on the next crest and offered Cassie and Lisa a drink from a water bottle before taking a long pull himself. Cassie looked back at the way they had come. Treetops and underbrush. There's hardly any path at all, she thought, but it will be easier going back. We just go down.

Charles pointed to the other side of the crest. "There's a Jeep over there, where the road ends," he said.

Cassie and Lisa stared at the small automobile. The turnaround was fairly open, but the Jeep was half hidden in thick foliage. Lisa, unusually quiet, sat listlessly on the ground. "Maybe someone else is going to Maiden's Hill," she said. "Only they had enough sense to drive."

Charles nodded. "They probably left their car there and are walking the rest of the way. Or maybe it broke down."

Cassie said nothing, but the sight of the car made her worry. Could someone be following them? What about Professor Ornard? Did he have the ring? Even if he did, he didn't have the secret panel and its clue. But he could easily have found out where the Nobre Plantation was, followed them there, and waited for them. And those two men who had beat up Jacques? What about them?

They passed the turnaround and pushed on, incline after incline. Lisa brushed a dirty hand across her forehead. "Let's have lunch here," she said. "I'm starving."

"It shouldn't be much farther," Charles said, peering at thinning trees on the far side of the track. "There's a sign," he shouted. "Come on, we'll get up there and have lunch."

They clambered, on hands and knees, up the last

steep slope. At the crest, they left the forest behind and stood on a windswept meadow. Cassie gazed in wonder at the majestic beauty surrounding her. Westward, the lush wooded hills tumbled into the sparkling Caribbean. Eastward, the mountains rose, bright in the midday sun.

Cassie turned from the view of the sea far below and, shielding her eyes with her hands, stared across the sun-swept meadows at the towering mountain. She shivered, seeing in her mind's eye the story of Maiden's Hill reenacted. The maiden, dressed in wedding finery, flowers woven in her long black hair, watching her future husband run across the field, his muscles rippling beneath his smooth brown skin.

On the other side of the mountain was the tameless ocean. And on that particular day there was not only the fierce, savage ocean but also the fierce, savage Caribs, who swept down and destroyed the maiden's world.

Charles's voice broke into Cassie's reverie. "Cassie, you look like you're in a trance. Come on. Before Lisa eats everything."

"I thought the food was supposed to be good on this island," grumbled Lisa, sitting under the single tree that graced the meadow, gnawing at a chicken leg. "I think this is last night's rejects."

Charles tossed her an orange. "Eat this. At least there's plenty of fruit."

Cassie hugged herself. "How can you guys eat? Here we are, on Maiden's Hill. And the cave. I bet that's the entrance, up there." She pointed to a dark area in the mountainside.

Charles thrust a banana in her hand. "You'd better eat something, Cassie, before we go in."

"Go in?" Lisa choked on an orange section. "Who said anything about going in?"

Charles laughed. "We didn't come all this way just to eat lunch, Lisa."

"But, what—what about the ghost? I'm not going in there. No way," said Lisa, shaking her head so hard, her ponytail whipped her face.

Cassie peeled the thick yellow skin of the banana. "I thought you didn't believe in ghosts, Lisa. Anyway, it's daytime. And the ghost only comes out at night."

Lisa wiped her sticky hands in the warm, dry grass. "But it will be dark in there. We won't be able to see anything."

"Ta-da," sang Charles, reaching into his knapsack and pulling out a flashlight.

"Good thinking, Charles. I never gave that a thought. What else do you have in there?" Cassie asked, watching Charles pull out a pickax, hand shovel, and small book. "What's the book for?"

"I got it from the library this morning while you were still sleeping. It's about lava caves. I got the other stuff in a storage shed Madame Bonne showed me."

"Now we're all set," said Cassie, giving him an excited hug. A sudden anxiety swept through her. "Charles, do you think we'll really find it?"

Charles, too, became serious. "I hope so, Cassie."

They sat, Indian style, in the fresh-smelling grass and finished lunch. Cassie swallowed the last bite of banana. Suddenly she decided to tell Charles and Lisa about last night. She took a deep breath and plunged into the story.

Charles's eyes never left her face, his brow creasing in a troubled scowl. Lisa, her voice quivering, said, "Those men. Who do you suppose they were? Do you think that was their car? That they followed us?"

"No. I'm sure they left last night. Anyway, why would they follow us?" said Cassie, massaging her aching calf muscles.

Charles pulled out the hand shovel and dug a hole to bury the lunch remnants. Cassie, shielding her eyes from the blinding sun, walked toward the mountain, scanning its surface.

Clouds drifted in, blocking the hot rays. Cassie looked up, no longer able to see the top of the mountain. She felt a surge of urgency. Night came quickly on the island, and here in the mountains, night meant cold.

Charles caught up with her, Lisa trudging behind him. Charles turned, his eyes sweeping the field and wooded hills. He looked up at the sky, then at his watch. "We got a later start than we should have. We have no idea how long it will take us in the cave."

"But it's the only time we have, Charles. The ship leaves tomorrow."

They scrambled up rock and loose stone to a more level ledge. The cave entrance, north of the lone tree, shaped like an egg lying on its side, loomed before them. Cassie glanced back over the field, unable to still a nagging sense of anxiety. Seeing Lisa's pinched face, she wished she hadn't told her about last night.

Cassie's heart beat expectantly as she walked into the wide entrance. Quickly, her mood changed from anxiety to anticipation. The Jeweled Jesu was near. She felt it in her bones.

Inside, smooth walls soared upward. They followed the ascending slope of the passage, which abruptly turned right into cool darkness. Charles snapped on the flashlight, playing its strong beam around the cavern.

"It's so big and dark." Lisa's voice sounded hollow.

Charles swept the light along the ground. "Watch your step," he warned. "According to the book, there's a vadose canyon to our left. We have to stay close together. Nobody wander away."

"A vadose canyon?" said Cassie. "What's that?"

"It's formed when the lava melts into the floor of the cave," said Charles. "The molten lava also forms falls, like a waterfall. Sometimes, it seals off part of the passage."

"I'm not going any farther," Lisa announced. "I'm going back to the entrance. I'll wait for you there."

Cassie swiveled toward her. "Lisa, stay with us. Don't you want to be there when we find the Jeweled Jesu?"

Lisa snorted. "The Jeweled Jesu! I think you're both crazy. How could you find anything in this black hole? And I bet that statue isn't even here. I'm going back. I'm not going any farther," she repeated, an edge of hysteria in her voice.

"Lisa." Charles's voice stopped her.

"What?" She stood poised, ready to run.

"It's all right if you don't come. But promise you'll wait at the entrance."

"Don't worry. I wouldn't try to go down that mountain by myself."

"Promise?" Charles called.

"Promise," she answered, throwing the word back over her shoulder.

Cassie watched her go. "I wish she'd stay," she murmured. She thought of Lisa's accusation: "You're just jealous because your father's my father now." Was it true? She pushed the disquieting thought away.

Charles took Cassie's arm and led her along. "Come on. If we're right, this should lead to a second room. Then we'll have to search for the secret room."

Cassie's heart bounded to her throat. The secret room. The Jeweled Jesu.

Slowly, they inched their way through the black cavern, Charles sweeping the sides and floor with his light. Cassie's eyes followed the light. The passage seemed at most fifty feet wide, running parallel to the side of the mountain rather than deeper into it. Cassie became aware of a sense of sorrow and foreboding. It seemed palpable—with a life of its own.

After a time, the air felt thicker and reeked of a stifling odor. Cassie's head ached, and a hard knot settled in her chest. The light flickered, paled.

Charles shook the flashlight, and it beamed again. He put his free arm around Cassie and gave her a reassuring squeeze. "Don't worry," he said. "I've got extra batteries."

Cassie leaned against him, welcoming his warmth. "I'm glad you think of those things," she said.

Charles's light played over a waterfall of solidified lava. "A lava cataract," he explained. "It blocks half the passage."

Cassie's shoulders ached with tension, and blood pounded in her temples. She steeled herself to go through the narrow passage, longing for the wide open meadow so far behind them.

"This must be the second room, the second X on the map," Charles's voice echoed eerily. His light barely penetrated the absolute dark.

Cassie gagged. "What is that awful smell?"

"Sulfur," said Charles. "It sure is powerful, isn't it?"

They stood, waiting to get their bearings. Cassie, hand over nose and mouth, heard nothing in the thick silence but their breathing. Charles sent the light quickly around the area. "The incline looks steeper and the passage narrower," he said, breaking the silence.

Cassie, clinging to a strap on Charles's knapsack, followed him up the passage. Her sneakers, wet through, made small squishing sounds.

Charles stopped abruptly. The flashlight's uncertain light circled the wider area, illuminating solid wall. Charles cleared his throat. "This must be the second room," he said, his voice low.

Cassie felt the hair at the back of her neck prickle. "There's something strange about this place," she whispered, reaching for Charles's hand with trembling fingers.

Charles gripped her hand. "Don't let your imagination run wild, Cassie," he said. "Now, if we're right, and this is what my grandfather meant as the second room, there has to be an opening to a third room."

His light swept the floor, checking for lava canyons, then circled the solid wall, going back to a towering mass of rock. "That must be a lava-seal," he murmured.

"It looks the same as the lava-falls," said Cassie.

"It is. Only it completely blocks the passage. Unless . . ."

"Unless there's some way around, behind, or through it," said Cassie eagerly.

They explored the seal from left to right, probing every crevice with the light. Dirty, tired, and cold, they sat staring dejectedly at the lava seal.

Cassie took the light from Charles and played it up and down the mass. Suddenly, she jumped up. "Charles, we've been looking for an opening at ground level. What if there's an opening farther up, behind one of those rocks?"

Charles's voice echoed her excitement. "I'll climb up and have a look."

"We'll both go," said Cassie.

"Some of those rocks are loose, Cassie. It would be better if you wait down here."

"No way, Charles. I'm going with you."

Cassie held the light for Charles as he found footholds to the next level. She then handed him the light, and he illuminated the trail for her.

Standing on a narrow ledge, leaning against the rock, Cassie shivered, goose bumps rising on her arms. "It's so cold. I'm freezing," she said through chattering teeth.

"How can you be cold after that climb? The sweat's pouring off me. Are you sure you want to go on?"

"I'm sure."

Cautiously, they made their way around the face of the cliff, poking and probing behind every outcropping.

"We're nearly to the end of this ledge," said

Charles. "I bet we have to climb higher."

"We're close, Charles. I just know it."

A large rock blocked their way. "Last spot," Charles said, flashing the light behind the rock formation. "Cassie." His voice rang out. "There's an opening. This is it. The way to the third room."

Cassie followed Charles through the narrow gap. His probing light flickered, brightened, then died. "Time for those new batteries," he said.

Cassie pressed against a rock, hardly aware of the sounds Charles made rustling through the knapsack, opening the package of batteries, and unscrewing the flashlight head. The atmosphere around her seemed to thicken; the temperature dropped. Again she shivered with cold, and the hairs on her arms prickled. A sense of great sorrow filled her.

"Cassie." Charles's voice came to her as though through a fog. "Cassie, don't you hear me? Hold these batteries for me."

When Cassie took the batteries from Charles, he said, "Your hands feel like blocks of ice."

"Charles," Cassie whispered, "don't you feel it?"

"Feel what?"

"There's someone else here—someone who's very sad."

"Cassie, you're giving me the creeps. Come on, the light's fixed."

"It's not scary, Charles. It's . . . it's kind of comforting."

Charles searched her face in the shadowy light. His voice catching, he murmured, "You're as pale as a ghost." Taking her arm and speaking in a louder voice, he said, "Let's see where we are."

His light searched the area. They stood on a ledge two feet above a passage that sloped steeply upward. The floor and walls formed a ten-foot-wide trench; the ceiling vaulted above them.

Cassie shook her head, as though to clear it; then, following Charles, she jumped to the stone floor. They climbed the ascending passage, which narrowed, then widened, then narrowed once again. Abruptly, they faced a solid wall.

"A lava-seal," said Charles, "the end of the road. But it seems lighter, and there's a draft of fresh air." He swung the light up, and, craning their necks, they studied the small opening high above them.

"Do you think we could get out that way?" asked Cassie.

"Maybe you could. It looks too narrow for me," said Charles. A gust of wind threw tiny particles into their faces. Charles wiped his eyes, then scuffed pieces of rock with his foot. "I wonder how long that crack has been there. It looks like the roof is starting to cave in. There's lots of loose stone."

"Then this is the end of the trail," said Cassie. "And, we . . ."

"And we didn't find the Jeweled Jesu," Charles finished.

Cassie put her arms about him and hugged him. "But we tried. We sure tried," she said.

Charles rested his chin on her head. Then, his hands gripping her arms tightly, he said, "Maybe we missed it. Maybe it's buried. We'll search every inch of this place before we leave."

He slowly washed the floor with his light as they retraced their steps. Close to the wider area, the light disclosed another passage.

"How did we miss that?" said Cassie.

"It's set at an angle. And it's so narrow, you'd never notice it on the way in," said Charles excitedly.

He edged in sideways into the inky crevice, Cassie close behind him. Suddenly he cried, "Oh, my God," and stepped back, crushing Cassie's foot and squeezing her against the rough wall.

"What is it?" she asked, rubbing her shoulder.

"A . . . a skeleton," Charles whispered.

"A skeleton? Let me see," said Cassie, pushing against him.

Cautiously, Charles stepped forward into a small alcove. His shaky light fell on the skull of the skeleton.

Cassie clung to Charles's arm. "The girl. The Arawak maiden. It must be her skeleton," she said, her voice trembling.

Charles reached out as though to touch the skeleton but jerked his hand back. His light traveled over the pale bones. "Whoever it was suffered a broken leg. You can see the break right there," he said, steadying the light on the upper-right thighbone.

Cassie felt tears stinging her eyes. She swallowed hard and said, "Charles, it must be the Arawak girl. Just think, all those centuries—entombed in here. . . . It's her presence I feel," she murmured.

They stood quietly for a moment, Charles's arm around Cassie's shoulders.

"I was just thinking about something I read—that ghosts may be like a footprint that some event has left imprinted in time. That's what the maiden's ghost is—a footprint of the Arawak massacre, and of her lost love."

"Come on, Cassie," said Charles, sounding matter-of-fact. "Just because we found this skeleton doesn't mean there's really a ghost."

Cassie gnawed at her lower lip and watched as

Charles flashed the light upward, scanning the claustrophobic walls. No matter what Charles says, she thought, I know the Arawak maiden's ghost is here.

Charles's searching light stopped at a shallow ledge. On it rested a metal box. He pulled it down and placed it on the floor, away from the skeleton. With the pickax, he pried the lid open and shone the light on its contents.

Cassie gasped. There in the box lay the Jeweled Jesu, its silver tarnished but its thirteen gems glowing richly in the dim light.

Drawing her gaze from the glowing treasure, Cassie looked at Charles. "Now you can fulfill your grandfather's wish and return the Jeweled Jesu to the church," she whispered.

Tears glistened in Charles's eyes. "Yes, I can fulfill my grandfather's wish."

Chapter 13

With the Jeweled Jesu in Charles's knapsack, they began their journey back. They squeezed through the fissure to the other side of the lava-fall, then, cautiously, holding the light for each other, made their way down. Cassie's heart raced with excitement. She couldn't wait to show Lisa the Jeweled Jesu. Darkness lifted as they neared the entrance, and Cassie walked ahead of Charles.

"Cassie, take it easy. Don't forget that canyon," he called.

She hurried back to his side and squeezed his arm. "Oh Charles, we found it! We really found it!"

Charles clicked off the light. "Hold it, Cassie. Before we go out there, I just want to tell you that, uh, that I'm really glad you were on the ship."

Cassie's cheeks burned. Now, she was in no hurry to leave the cave. "I'm glad I was on the ship too," she whispered.

Charles bent his mouth to hers. His kiss was warm and tender. Cassie wrapped her arms around his neck. Her heart sang.

Arms around each other, half running, half skipping, they rounded the curve that led to the egg-shaped entrance, where dim light from the westering sun filtered in.

"Cassie! Charles!" Lisa's voice was a hoarse whisper. "I didn't think you'd ever get back. What took you so long? It's so late and—"

"Lisa!" Cassie hugged her jubilantly. "We found it! We found the Jeweled Jesu! Just wait till you see it!"

"Cassie, be quiet. He'll hear you," sobbed Lisa.

"Who will hear me?" asked Cassie. "What are you talking about?"

Lisa grabbed Cassie's arm. Her hands felt damp and cold. "I was outside for a while. I fell asleep. When I woke up, the professor was standing there, staring at me. So I ran into the cave."

"The professor?" said Cassie. "You mean . . . he

followed us?" Gazing at Lisa, she murmured, "That must have been his Jeep. He must have been here all the time. Hiding. Spying on us. Watching us eat lunch."

"That guy gives me the creeps," said Charles, swinging his knapsack off and setting it on the ground. "But if he knows we're in here, how come he's out there? Why didn't he follow you in, Lisa?"

"I don't know, but I'm sure glad he didn't. He scared me. He looked sort of crazy. When I ran in here, he yelled something about waiting us out," wailed Lisa.

"Ah, so you're back," said the professor as though he were greeting them on the ship. He stood just at the beginning of the curve, limned against the setting sun. "I thought I heard triumphant cries. Now you can show me, as well as Lisa, what you found." He rubbed his knuckled left ring finger against his right wrist. In his right hand, he held a gun.

Cassie felt everything go quiet within her. She heard Charles, standing beside her, draw in a sharp breath and Lisa scurry behind them.

"I will use this if necessary," warned the professor. "Now, slow and easy, slide that knapsack over here, Charles."

Charles hesitated, then pushed the knapsack forward with his foot.

Cassie caught the strap with her foot and yanked it back. "If you want to see what's in here, come and get it," she yelled.

"Cassie." Charles's voice was a hoarse whisper. "He's got a gun! Don't fool around."

Philippe Ornard stretched his arm forward and clicked the trigger. "You'd be smart to listen to him for a change," he threatened. "I've waited too long for this. The Jeweled Jesu belongs to me."

"It doesn't belong to you. Why should it belong to you?" said Cassie, anger giving her courage.

"It belongs to me, I tell you." The professor's voice rose, then leveled off. He spoke quietly, dispassionately. "Ever since I can remember, the story of the Jeweled Jesu has consumed me. I've spent years studying and writing about jewels. Years. And what do I have to show for it? Nothing. But now it's my turn. Just one of those gems is worth a fortune."

Charles bent and grabbed the knapsack, holding it against his chest. "You mean you'd break it apart? Sell it off—jewel by jewel? You said that would be sacrilegious."

Professor Ornard threw back his head and laughed—a harsh, mirthless sound. Gesturing with the gun, he commanded, "Give that here."

"When did you start following us?" asked Cassie, stalling for time.

"I came to the plantation late last night. Slept in my car. Most uncomfortable. I figured you brats would lead me to the treasure today. And it's good you did! After what I paid Larson for this ring"—he reached into his pocket and held up the ring—"all that money—and nothing in it." He hurled the ring and the loose stone at them.

Cassie felt a sharp impact against her knee. She crouched and searched for the pieces with her hand.

Philippe Ornard's voice was filled with cold fury. "As soon as I saw the interior plate was missing, I knew you two had whatever clue was in there."

"So you got the ring," said Cassie, thrusting the pieces in Charles's hand. "Larson told us there were other bidders for it."

"Others? There was one I know of. Your dear cousin, Jacques, Charles. But he didn't get it. Lack of funds, I suppose. But I do have him to thank for putting me on the trail."

"What do you mean?" asked Charles sharply.

The professor, in a self-congratulatory tone,

said, "Jacques, you know, is a bit of a drinker and a gambler. Not a good combination. But thanks to his loose tongue, I heard him in a bar last Friday rambling on about his Uncle Jerome and a young cousin he had never met—a cousin who was sailing on the *Seabird* and bringing with him a clue to some treasure's whereabouts. It seems he'd overheard an argument between his father and his uncle. No one else was paying any attention to him. But when I heard him talk about treasure and a feud going back many years, I knew I had to follow up on it. Missed my transportation that night. Luckily, I got someone early Saturday morning to fly me to Miami. It was important I board the *Seabird* and meet this young cousin."

Charles, Cassie, and Lisa had been inching their way backward into the dark recesses of the cave as the professor rambled on.

He's so smug and proud of all his planning, thought Cassie. What else can I ask him to keep him talking? He won't come in here. I just know he won't. "I don't understand why you missed your Friday night plane," she prompted.

"Why because I had to visit old Jerome Nobre and verify Jacques's tip," he explained.

A strangled cry came from Charles. "My grandfather. You killed my grandfather."

Cassie reached out and grabbed his shirt as he sprang toward the professor. She heard the material rip. "Charles, don't," she hissed.

"Your grandfather was fine when I left him," said the professor coolly. "Maybe I had to rough him up a little—the old fool wouldn't tell me anything—but he was alive when I left."

The last rays of the setting sun that filtered into the cave entrance behind the professor faded. Cassie, in the half-light, saw him look toward the entrance, then jerk his head back. He shouted, his voice tinged with fear, "Get out here, now, or I'll shoot."

"Why don't you come in, Professor?" Cassie taunted. "Or are you afraid, afraid of the maiden? She's in here, you know. Charles and I saw her. She's our protector."

"Come out here and I'll go easy on you. Larson should be here soon. He's with me. He went back to get supplies—food and flashlights—just in case he has to go in there after you. And he'll get rid of you kids once and for all. Then you can roam around in that cave with the maiden forever!" he shouted, and laughed hysterically.

He raised the gun, clicked the trigger, and a bullet whizzed by Cassie's ear as she, Charles, and Lisa fled farther into the cave.

Chapter 14

The three stumbled through the pitch-black cavern. "Hang on to me," shouted Charles, leading them to the right. "We have to stay away from that canyon."

Gunshots and Philippe Ornard's screaming voice echoed behind them. "Come out here, you fools, come out! You think the maiden will protect you? You're crazy! No one spends a night in there and comes out alive! She sees to that!"

Lisa stumbled and grasped Cassie's arm to keep from falling. "Did you see any snakes before? Did you really see that ghost? I don't want to go any deeper."

"I think it's safe to turn the light on now,

Charles," said Cassie. "The professor won't follow us, anyway."

"Okay," said Charles, "let's stop here and get our bearings." He clicked the flashlight on, and the three of them looked at one another in its pale beam.

After a moment, Charles asked, "Why do you think the professor won't come into the cave, Cassie?"

"I don't care why," said Lisa. "Just so long as he doesn't."

"Because he's so superstitious," explained Cassie. "He's always rubbing that ankh of his. And remember when he first talked about Maiden's Hill? He looked really spooked. I knew then he believed in ghosts."

Lisa tugged on Cassie's arm. "But, Cassie, what if there is a ghost in here? Aren't you afraid of it?"

"Cassie thinks there is," said Charles. "When we saw the skeleton—"

"Skeleton?" shrieked Lisa. "There's a skeleton in here? I'm not going another step." She folded her arms across her chest, squared her jaw, and backed against the cavern wall.

Cassie reached out and touched Lisa's arm. "There is a skeleton, Lisa. But it can't hurt us. It's the maiden's skeleton. I just know it is. She was trapped by a rock. One of her leg bones is crushed."

Lisa covered her face and whimpered. "I want to go home."

"Listen, Lisa. The maiden's ghost is our friend. There's nothing in here for us to be afraid of."

"No," said Charles. "But there's plenty outside to be afraid of, and when Larson—"

"I wonder if the professor was telling the truth about Larson?" Cassie interrupted. "When Larson had me stranded on that rock, he said he was taking off after he sold the ring . . . because it didn't have the panel in it."

"So you think the professor's lying?" asked Charles.

"He could be. After all, when he said he followed us last night, he didn't mention Larson. He probably just wants us to think someone is coming to help him . . . but then, Larson did figure out the panel must be a clue to something. Before I told him we'd lost it, he said he was going to make sure whoever he sold it to shared the treasure with him."

"We're stuck in here," Lisa sobbed. "We can't get out, and if Larson does come—"

"But your uncle, Charles. When we don't show up for dinner, he'll—"

Charles, looking at Lisa, shook his head slightly. "This morning, Madam Bonne said my uncle would be late tonight."

"We're going to starve to death. I just know we are," sobbed Lisa. "And nobody will ever find us—not till we're skeletons."

"Calm down, Lisa," said Charles, giving her shoulders a reassuring squeeze. "There is another way out. We have to climb a lava-falls to get to it. It's just past where we found the Jeweled Jesu." He swept the walls of the cavern with the light. "We'd better get going. It will take a while to get there."

Cassie thought of the crevice high in the ceiling of the last passage. Could they get out that way? It was high up and looked very narrow. But it was worth a try. And, even if they couldn't get out and Larson did come, they'd be safely hidden in the secret room.

Gagging from the heavy sulfur odor, they made their way to the first lava-fall. Lisa stared at the nearly perpendicular wall. "There's no way I'm climbing up there," she said.

"It's not as bad as it looks," said Cassie. "I'll go first, then you, and Charles will come last."

Charles tied a rope about Cassie's waist. "Okay, Cassie, up you go," he said. "Watch carefully,

Lisa, so you'll know where the best footholds are."

Finally, the three of them stood outside the narrow gap. Cassie squeezed through and reached back for Lisa's hand. Lisa took a deep breath and tried to wriggle through. "I'm stuck. I'll never get through here."

"Hold your breath, Lisa. I'm going to give you a push," said Charles.

Lisa popped through the opening. Charles came next, and the three of them stood on the ledge that led into the inner chamber. Cassie felt an icy breath and a thickening of the atmosphere. The hair on the back of her neck prickled, but a sense of calm flowed through her. "Do you feel it?" she whispered. "The maiden is here."

"That's not funny, Cassie. And I don't feel anything except scratched and bruised," said Lisa, rubbing her arms.

One by one they jumped the two feet to the passage below.

"Where's the skeleton?" asked Lisa. "I don't want to see it."

"You won't have to," said Charles. "It's in a hidden room. We'll go right by it."

Cassie led the way up the ascending passage. Suddenly she stopped, and the others bumped into her. "Look," she whispered, "the maiden." Ahead of her, a milky figure drifted into the crevice that led to the alcove.

Lisa's grip of Cassie's hand was viselike. Charles laughed nervously and said, "You're seeing things, Cassie. It's just the moonlight coming through the opening at the end of the passage."

Cassie didn't argue with him. But moonlight wouldn't show this far in, and it wouldn't have a human shape. She knew that.

Cassie paused by the fissure. What would she see if she went in there? What would happen? She shivered, then, knowing she had promised Lisa she wouldn't have to see the skeleton, she moved on. At the end of the passage, Cassie gazed up at the hazy outlet. A cold ribbon of night air flowed down on them.

Charles, moving the light back and forth across the opening, said, "It's freezing in here. Once the sun goes down, it gets cold in the mountains, but then, it's always cold in caves, anyway."

Cassie didn't say anything, but she knew the cold she felt wasn't from the night air.

Lisa, loosening her grip on Cassie's hand, snorted. "That's the way out? You've got to be kidding. It's too small and it's too high. I could hardly get through that other opening. I'll never get through there." She sank to the floor and buried her face in her hands.

Cassie had been expecting an outburst of accusations from Lisa, but none came. Lisa was right. No way could she get through that outlet.

"I'll give it a try," said Charles, handing the light to Cassie.

"I'm the only one who'll fit, Charles," said Cassie, refusing to take the light. She knelt beside Lisa and gave her a quick hug. "I can get out, Lisa, and I'll get help."

Lisa lifted her head. Her face was pale in the dim light. "You'd have to go down the mountain by yourself . . . in the dark," she whispered.

Cassie nodded, wondering if she could find her way back.

"Cassie?" Lisa's voice was small. "I'm sorry about last night . . . and the way I acted on the boat. I—"

Cassie interrupted her. "We've both been kind of silly," she said. "We'll have more fun on the trip back."

"Yeah—the trip back . . ." Lisa's voice trailed off.

Charles rustled in his knapsack. "Hey, come on, Lisa. Cassie will make it and get us out of here. Cheer up! Cassie, I'll hold the light for you, then send it up. You'll need it in that jungle."

He tied the rope around her waist again, then grabbed her in a fierce hug and held her against him.

Cassie, not trusting her voice, nodded. Grasping at nubs on the coarse wall, searching for footholds, she started the climb, finding her way more by feel than from Charles's flickering light. Small stones and dirt sifted into her eyes and mouth. She felt blood ooze from her scraped fingertips.

Suddenly, her foot slipped, and she slid downward. Hands and feet searched frantically for holds. Her feet found a small ledge, and, heart racing, she leaned into the wall. She listened to loosened stones thundering down from rock to rock.

"Are you all right?" shouted Charles.

"I'm okay. I'll make it," said Cassie, forcing her voice to sound strong. She waited for her heart to stop hammering, for her breathing to return to normal. Not daring to look down, she slowly worked her way to the top, then scraped through the crevice.

She lay on bracken-covered rock and breathed in great gulps of the night air. Rolling onto her stomach, she called to Charles, "Okay, send up the light."

She pulled up the knapsack, felt it snag against a rock, and yanked it free. She took the flashlight out, searched on the ground for a rock, and placed it on top of the knapsack. It would make a good marker when she returned . . . if they needed to go in this way. When she returned, she thought, when she returned . . .

Clutching the flashlight in a sweaty, bleeding hand, kneeling on scraped knees, she called, "I've got the light. I'm off."

Charles and Lisa's voices drifted up: "Good luck."

They were depending on her. Somehow she'd have to find her way down the mountain for help. And she had to hurry. Maybe the professor had lied about Larson. Maybe he hadn't. She wasn't sure. But she was sure of a premonition of danger.

Chapter 15

Cassie, feeling small and alone in immense darkness, huddled on the side of the mountain. Clouds shifted, and the moon momentarily lightened the black night. A gust of wind swept a brittle leaf against her face. She shivered and stumbled to her feet.

Where was she? Where was the professor? Would he see the light if she turned it on? She didn't dare take the chance. She thought of the long trek up the steep, overgrown path this morning. How could she find that path?

Something scurried by. What kind of animals are out here? she wondered. She pushed down the panic rising in her throat. A plan. She needed a plan.

If she could just find the tree where they had had lunch. Then, at least, she'd know what direction to go in. Where was she in relationship to that tree and the entrance to the cave? In the cave, they had journeyed south and upward. It had seemed a long way. But, considering climbing lava-flows, maybe they hadn't gone such a far distance.

Cassie started northwest down the steep incline. Her foot snagged on something. Yanking it free, she fell and rolled over sharp stones into a bush. She got shakily to her feet and checked her weight on her ankle. No break. Just a little sore. The wind, carrying the damp smell of rain, whistled by her ears.

It just can't rain! It can't! she thought. "I've got to get an idea of where I am," she murmured, clicking the flashlight on. She focused the light at her feet, keeping its telltale illumination near her. More bravely, she scanned its light over the mountainside, searching the meadow below for its lone tree.

"Who's there? Who's there?"

Cassie snapped off the light and hit the ground. Professor Ornard. How close was he? Had he seen her? She lay frozen on the mountainside for what seemed an eternity. Gradually, she got to her knees. She had come farther north than she'd realized. Afraid to stand to her full height for fear the clouds would shift and the moon reveal her, she scuttled back but continued downward. At last she lay on the soft grass of the meadow. On such an open space, she should be able to see the deeper darkness of a tree, but nothing. She could distinguish nothing. Not daring to turn on the light, she waited for the clouds to part and show her the tree.

Once I find the tree, I can find my way back, she thought. I'll have to follow the road. It will take a lot longer, but at least I won't get lost in that jungle.

The moisture-laden wind picked up and tore the clouds. Cassie breathed a sigh of relief and, keeping low to the ground, ran to the tree. She sank beneath it, feeling the soft dirt where Charles had buried the lunch scraps. Charles. A lump formed in her throat. She had to get help. What if Larson was really coming? He and the professor together. They would do anything to get the Jeweled Jesu.

Cassie had to go down the path to reach the turnaround where they had seen the professor's car. Not daring to turn on her light, grabbing hold of branches, slipping on stones, she slowly felt her way down. A sudden thought jolted her: What if Larson was already there? What if, at this very moment, he was stalking Charles and Lisa?

She reached the turnaround. Only one car. No one else had come. There was time. Pushing herself on, ignoring the pains shooting through her shins, unaware of an occasional splat of rain, she ran down the road, slowing to a walk only when her breath came in gasps and pains ripped through her side.

She lost track of time, feeling as though she were running in a dream. A motor accelerated, and lights flashed around a curve. Cassie, startled as a deer, froze, then darted into the woods. Brakes jammed; wheels screeched to a halt. A door opened and slammed.

Cassie, heart racing, ran blindly farther into the woods. She dropped the flashlight. It lay in the thick underbrush like a one-eyed animal.

"Cassie. Cassie. Stop. Come back here."

Cassie heard the voice and stopped, a surge of relief flooding through her. It wasn't Larson. It was Jacques.

He caught up with her, a flashlight in one hand. With the other, he grabbed her upper arm.

"Jacques," Cassie babbled. "Charles and Lisa

are in the cave. The professor is at the entrance with a gun. I got out through the other opening, but—"

"They're in the cave? Still looking for the Jeweled Jesu? When Maria told me you'd gone to Maiden's Hill, I knew that was it. That's where my foolish old uncle hid it."

Cassie felt numb. She'd been so relieved it wasn't Larson. She'd forgotten the professor had said Jacques was the other bidder for the ring. "I . . . I thought you were Larson," she stammered.

Jacques snorted. "Larson. Larson's not going anywhere, that double-dealing creep."

Cassie's hand tingled beneath Jacques's blood-stopping grasp. Scenes from last night flooded her mind. Those two men, hitting him again and again. "What do you mean he's not going anywhere? Who were those men who beat you up last night? Why were you in your uncle's office?" she gasped.

"Those two thugs want money, little Miss Snoop, and I'd hoped to find some in that office. But no dice. Lady luck wasn't with me. If I don't get money soon, I'm as good as dead." He pivoted her around, dropped her arm, and pushed a short-barreled gun in her back. "Get in the car. You take me to the Jeweled Jesu and nobody gets hurt." Cassie, planting her feet firmly, didn't budge.

"What happened to Larson?" she asked.

Jacques pushed the gun against her back. "Nosy, aren't you? Get moving, Cassie, or you won't be able to."

Her tears mingling with the rain that now fell steadily through the black night, Cassie staggered toward the road. She and Charles had been so close—so close to realizing his grandfather's dream. She couldn't go back with Jacques. She couldn't give in. Just before she reached the road, she lurched to her left and floundered into the woods.

A gunshot rang out. Wet branches whipped her face, arms, and legs. Jacques crashed through the underbrush, shouting, "You can't get away from me. You'll get lost in this jungle."

Cassie plunged on, long after the sounds of Jacques's pursuit had died. Finally, exhausted, she sank to the ground. Cold rain dripped from the trees and crept down her neck. Jacques would go to Maiden's Hill. He and the professor would fight. He had said Larson wasn't going anywhere. What did he mean? But Jacques in the cave was more of a threat than Larson. Jacques would know about lava-caves. He would know to look for breaks in a lava-fall. And if he found Charles and Lisa . . .

Numb and too weary to move, Cassie leaned against the wet bark of a tree. The wind moaned through the treetops, unleashing leaf-trapped rain. The reeking scent of decaying vegetation stole up from the moist ground. Her eyes strained wide against the thick darkness. Disoriented, she didn't know which way to go.

Frigid air brushed by her. Then, a subtle lightening of the pitch-dark appeared through the trees. A feeling of calm settled over Cassie. She rose and walked toward the lighter area. Maybe it was a clearing. Maybe it was the road, and the moon was shining through a break in the leaden sky. She reached the spot and found herself still surrounded by forest.

The light, stronger now, beckoned from a distance. As though in a dream, Cassie followed it. Each time she reached it, it disappeared, only to reappear farther on. Soon she realized she was on the path they had followed that morning. The light beckoned again and again, Cassie following it—down the path, over the road, and onto the next path. Finally, her head grazed a board. Rubbing her forehead, she realized she was at the first sign to Maiden's Hill that they had discovered that morning.

The rain stopped, and a sprinkling of pale stars shone in the sky. The light increased in intensity. Spellbound, Cassie watched as it materialized into a young girl. She felt an icy caress. Shivering, she watched the girl drift toward the trees, become formless, dimmer, until she disappeared. Cassie stood there a moment longer, then turned and ran down the road toward the plantation.

Chapter 16

Cassie splashed through puddles and sprinted along the muddy road. Finally, she stumbled up the long, rutted drive to the well-lit house. Her father paced back and forth on the veranda. When he saw her, he ran and scooped her into his arms, held her tight, and murmured, "Cassie. Cassie Lassie—my little girl. Thank God you're all right. I've been so worried. If anything happened to you . . ."

Cassie leaned a moment against her father's chest, then pushed away and cried, "We have to get up to Maiden's Hill. Charles and Lisa are in the cave and the professor and—"

The door opened, and Claude Nobre clattered

down the steps. "Charles and the young girl—they are all right?" he asked intently.

"They were when I left," said Cassie. Words tumbling over one another, she told them what had happened. She ended with, "Larson may be up there, too. I'm not sure. Jacques said . . ."

Claude Nobre's mouth tightened, and he shook his head. "No. Larson will not be there. When I called the police, they told me they had found him unconscious on the pier. When he came to, he kept talking about Jacques and how he had attacked him for a ring. He is in the hospital now."

Claude Nobre rambled on. "I was late getting home tonight. I arrived to find your father and Mrs. Hartt. They were worried when they called and you were not here. Then Maria told me you were not back and that Jacques had gone to look for you. I called the police to help search for you. They should be here soon." Running his fingers through his hair, he glanced toward the road.

"A police officer who is a friend of mine told me about my son. His debts . . . his gambling debts—they must be worse than I imagined . . . that he would do such a thing. . . . I am sorry, so sorry that he frightened you. . . ." he said, his voice trailing off.

Cassie tugged on his arm, "We have to hurry. We have to help Charles and Lisa." She pushed her damp hair from her face. "I'll show you where they are—"

"No," her father said decisively. "You tell us how to find them, then go in with Sonya. The housekeeper is trying to calm her down. She's nearly hysterical. You get into some warm, dry clothes. Mr. Nobre and I will go to Maiden's Hill. When the police get here, send them after us."

"No. I'm going with you. I promised. They're waiting for me, and I know just where they are." Cassie stared into her father's eyes, challenging him.

Her father returned her look, then, taking her arm, said, "Very well. We'll go together."

"Wait here," said Claude Nobre. "I will get the flashlights and supplies I have ready and tell Maria to inform the police to follow us."

Claude Nobre drove the Jeep up the winding road to Maiden's Hill, Cassie beside him, her father in the backseat. Windshield wipers swished back and forth, clearing the window of rain that spattered from overhanging trees.

Claude Nobre pulled into the turnaround and slammed on the brakes. Moonlight lit the clearing, and Cassie could see Jacques's car blocking the professor's. "Hurry," she called, jumping out of the Jeep and running toward the path.

She heard her father and Claude Nobre close behind her, then her father's loud whisper: "Cassie, slow down. You said they had guns."

But she couldn't slow down. Charles and Lisa were waiting in the dark cave, and Jacques . . . had he found them yet? Wet tree branches slapped against her face and arms, and soggy underbrush threatened to trip her. Would they ever get there?

Finally, they reached the moonlit meadow. All was silent. The lone tree, a towering silhouette, stood like a dark sentry.

"I'm sure the professor wouldn't go into the cave. He must still be out there. Unless Jacques—"

"Yes, unless Jacques surprised him," agreed Claude Nobre.

"If we go up and over, we can come down a little above the cave entrance and see what's happening," said Cassie. She led the two men up the mountain to its first leveling off and then north toward the cave entrance. Where was the professor? He wouldn't give up easily—Cassie was sure of that.

From their viewpoint above the cave entrance, the three of them trained their lights on the ground below. In the pool of light lay the professor, a dark splotch on his forehead.

The three scrabbled down the mountain to his side. James Hartt felt for a pulse. "He's alive. It doesn't look like a serious wound."

Moonlight glinting off metal caught Cassie's eye. Gingerly, she picked up the cold object and walked over to her father. "Here's his gun," she said, handing it to him with a shudder. She stared down at the professor.

His eyes flickered open and he returned her stare. "You. You," he muttered, his voice filled with hate.

Claude Nobre cut a length of rope from his supply and tied the man's hands behind his back. "There," he said, standing and brushing his hands, "he is ready for the police."

Cassie led them through the now familiar passage, her light sweeping the cavern walls and floor. How long would it take Jacques to find the secret room? Even if he'd been here before and knew about the second room, he'd still have to search for the secret passage. And he would probably start on the left, where she and Charles had, where the footholds were better.

Cassie knew they were approaching the lava-cataract when the overcoming smell of sulfur engulfed them. Gagging, hand over nose and mouth, she indicated the steep, narrower passage to the second room. Cassie felt the chill damp of the place but not the maiden's presence. Was she here?

"Is this the room? Where are they?" asked Claude Nobre in a hushed voice.

"There's no way out of here," said her father, sweeping his light around the room.

Cassie trained her light to the far upper right. "It's up there. You can't see it from down here." A flash of color showed in the beam's light. A yellow shirt. Jacques. "There he is. There's Jacques!" Cassie shouted.

A gunshot ricocheted off the cavern wall, starting a minor avalanche. Cassie jumped back, a jagged stone just missing her.

"Jacques, come down," called Claude Nobre. "You have done enough damage. Come down now."

"Stay put. All of you. I've got this gun and I won't hesitate to use it."

"Jacques, your uncle . . . your own uncle . . ." said Claude Nobre, his voice breaking. "How could you—"

"I didn't kill him," shouted Jacques. "I went to his office last Friday. Ornard had already been there. If Uncle Jerome had only cooperated! But he wouldn't. He wouldn't. When I left, he was alive; he was just having trouble breathing. It wasn't my fault he couldn't find his pills."

"And you did not help him? You did not call a doctor? You might as well have killed him!"

"He was an old man. He's dead! I'm not going to listen to any more of this. Stay where you are. Don't come up here." And Jacques disappeared behind the rocky projection.

"Light my way," said Cassie, thrusting her own light into a pocket. "I've been up here twice before today. I know the footholds."

"Cassie, wait. You can't go up there alone," her father commanded.

"I have a plan," Cassie called down from her perch on the first ledge. "It would take you and Mr. Nobre too long to get to the top. Just keep the light above me."

Cassie sidled behind the rocky projection, where the light beams from below could not follow. She stood on the ledge, engulfed in blackness. Afraid to turn on her own light, she waited for her eyes to adjust. Jacques knows about the other exit, she thought. But he doesn't know he can't get out that way. When Charles hears him coming, he'll probably hide with Lisa in the alcove, then . . .

Cassie jumped down from the ledge. Feeling the cold, rough walls with her hands, she inched up the ascending passage. She was almost to the alcove where the passage widened when she saw a wavering beam of light and heard footsteps. She froze, not daring to move, not daring to breathe.

The light fell on the passage to the alcove. "Ahh," Jacques murmured, "that's where they are."

Cassie saw his shadowy arm raise his gun. She bent and searched for a rock. If they could get the gun away from Jacques, they would have a chance.

The next few minutes were chaos. Light flooded the chamber just as Cassie heaved the rock. She heard the heavy thump of stone hitting flesh. Charles leaped out of the alcove and tackled Jacques, wrestling him to the ground. A police officer brushed past Cassie and joined the struggling forms. Another officer shoved a large flashlight into Cassie's hands, shouting, "Keep the light on Nobre."

The officers grabbed Jacques by the arms, handcuffed him, and started back toward the lava-seal. "Come on, kids," said one of the officers. "It will be a lot easier going down. We've got a rope-ladder."

Lisa, her hands icy, clung to Cassie. "The

skeleton . . . we had to go in there so Jacques wouldn't see us. Oh, Cassie, I want to go home," she sobbed.

"Dad is waiting for us at the bottom of the cliff," Cassie reassured her. "Your uncle is there, too, Charles. Would you go ahead with Lisa? I just want to . . ." Cassie gestured toward the alcove.

"We'll wait for you out here," said Charles. "Then we'll go back together."

The faint beam from Cassie's flashlight fell on the skeleton. She stood silently, bathed in an atmosphere of serenity. "Thank you, Arawak maiden," she whispered.

When they reached the lava-seal, one of the officers and Jacques were already down. Cassie and Charles waited their turn while the other officer encouraged Lisa to climb down the twisting rope-ladder.

Cassie felt a thickening of the atmosphere, and an icy chill ran down her back. Each little hair on her arms and the back of her neck prickled. She looked up the inky passage. A ghostly form appeared, materialized into a young girl, then faded away.

Chapter 17

Much later, they all gathered in the living room to enjoy coffee, hot chocolate, and sandwiches served by Maria Bonne. Cassie sat by Charles, who was polishing the Jeweled Jesu to luminous beauty, its gems flashing and radiating light.

Cassie leaned forward and traced the intricate carving with a finger. "I can't believe we did it, Charles," she said, wonder in her voice.

Charles stopped his polishing and looked into her eyes. Cassie felt her neck and face flush. "Hey, Cassie," he said softly. "With you spurring me on, we were sure to."

Cassie smiled. "My mother always says I'm determined—but then, so are you." She tapped the ring that once again hung on a chain around Charles's neck, its stone now taped in place. "Who knows? Maybe the ring had something to do with it. Remember—a lion's image engraved on a garnet will protect the wearer's honor and health, bring him honor, and guard him from danger in traveling."

Charles chuckled and said, "That's just superstition." His tone changed, and he became serious. "When I go home in August, I want to see you. I'll have two weeks before school starts. Maybe I can get to Maine."

A happy glow rushed through Cassie. "I'd like that—a lot," she said.

Cassie looked across the room to the couch. Her father's left arm supported Lisa, who slept against his chest. Sonya, who sat on Lisa's other side, rested her arm on James's as she stroked Lisa's hair. Cassie knew she and Sonya would never be close, but she'd have to accept her as her father's wife. Her father caught her eye, and they smiled at each other.

Cassie knew he loved her. He'd even called her by her old pet name—Cassie Lassie. But she had changed; she had outgrown that name, that time. Many things had changed. Her father would always be part of her, but never part of her family again. He loved her, but he loved Sonya and Lisa, too. Loving one person didn't stop you from loving another. She had learned that, she thought, putting her hand on Charles's arm.

Claude Nobre placed his coffee cup on a table and walked over to Cassie and Charles. He took the statue from Charles and held it up. The stones caught the light and radiated shafts of color. He began to speak, turning to include James and Sonya Hartt and Lisa.

"I wish to officially welcome my grand-nephew, Charles Nobre Reyes, to the Nobre Plantation. He and his friends have found the Jeweled Jesu, and it will now be returned to the church as it should have been many years ago." Sadness tinged his eyes and voice. "I cannot tell you how sorry I am that I fought with Jerome all those years. He was right. Of course, he was right. If only I had had the sense to see that."

He paused and gazed into the distance. "For years our plantation has not done well. Jerome said we were cursed, cursed for keeping the Jeweled Jesu. I told him that was nothing but superstition. Now I do not know. Perhaps, if I had listened to him, my son would be here with us tonight. Instead, he is in prison. He owes a great deal of money to men who kill if they are not paid. He has been under great pressure to repay those debts. Last night, when he called to ask me for money, I had no idea he wanted it to retrieve the ring in hopes of finding the Jeweled Jesu. Like me, he thought selling this sacred statue"—he looked at the shining statue he held—"would bring wealth—wealth and happiness. Like me, he was wrong.

"Both of us have committed crimes. I, through years of animosity toward my brother, and Jacques . . . Jacques let the pressures that surrounded him lead him to do things I find it hard to think him capable of."

Head bowed, he was quiet for a moment. Cassie suddenly realized the enormity of Claude Nobre's loss—not only had he lost his brother, he had also lost his son.

Claude Nobre looked up. His voice lighter, he said, "With Charles, I believe, will come a new prosperity for the Nobre Plantation and for the Nobre family. No more rifts between us. We are a family." He smiled at Charles and handed him the Jeweled Jesu. "Make it shine. Tomorrow, we will return it to its rightful place—the church."

Embarrassed, Charles took the statue and rubbed it furiously. Then he placed it on the coffee table, where its radiance seemed to fill the room. Charles reached for Cassie's hand, and they studied the luminous statue in silence.

After a moment, Charles turned to Cassie and said, "Cassie, how did you ever find your way down the mountain tonight?"

Cassie pulled her gaze from the shining statue and looked into his eyes. "Charles, it was the strangest thing. There really is a ghost of Maiden's Hill. I thought so when we were in the cave, but now I'm positive." In hushed tones, she told him about the light that had guided her through the dark woods to the path. "I would never have found it without her," she finished.

Charles, wide-eyed and intent, asked, "And you actually saw the form of a girl?"

Cassie nodded. "Yes, it was there for just a second or so. Then it faded away."

Charles's hand gripped hers tighter. "Awesome!" he whispered.

Cassie relaxed, relieved that Charles believed her. She had taken a chance telling him, afraid that he might laugh at her, but he hadn't. He had believed her.

Charles slipped his arm around Cassie's shoulders. She sighed and settled against him. Cassie wasn't sure what the future held—for her family in Maine, her new family, or even with Charles—but for now, this was enough.